Readers love
Z. ALLORA

Bent Not Broken

"My favourite quote is 'Life may have bent you a little but you are not broken.' It is so true for so many of us and one of several reasons as to why I recommend giving this story a go."
—Paranormal Romance Guild

"Very moving and inspiring OFY romance with incredibly well-rounded main characters. High on hurt/comfort and genuine emotions, very nuanced story-telling."
—Open Skye Book Reviews

The Great Wall

"I am very excited to check out the next books when they come out and definitely recommend this book and author."
—Rainbow Gold Reviews

"The growing love is sweet and strong despite all the difficulties."
—Diverse Reader

The Librarian's Rake

"If you are looking for a quick, relaxing read I would recommend picking this up."
—Just Love: Queer Book Reviews

"*The Librarian's Rake* by Z. Allora was an extremely sweet and cute book."
—Love Bytes

By Z. ALLORA

Bent Not Broken
The Craving
Illusions & Dreams
The Librarian's Rake
The Longest Night
Not Another Boy Band
Rocking Thin Ice

ENTWINED DREAMS
Lock and Key
Secured and Free

MADE IN CHINA
The Great Wall
The Temple of Heaven

Published by DREAMSPINNER PRESS
www.dreamspinnerpress.com

Z. ALLORA

NOT ANOTHER BOY BAND

DREAMSPINNER
PRESS

Published by
DREAMSPINNER PRESS

5032 Capital Circle SW, Suite 2, PMB# 279, Tallahassee, FL 32305-7886 USA
www.dreamspinnerpress.com

Not Another Boy Band
© 2021 Z. Allora

Cover Art
© 2021 Tiferet Design
http://www.tiferetdesign.com
Cover content is for illustrative purposes only and any person depicted on the cover is a model.

Trade Paperback ISBN: 978-1-64405-958-6
Digital ISBN: 978-1-64405-957-9
Trade Paperback published August 2021
First Edition
v. 1.0

Printed in the United States of America
∞
This paper meets the requirements of
ANSI/NISO Z39.48-1992 (Permanence of Paper).

To Tianyi
May your time speed by… until you have words again.

Acknowledgments

THANK YOU to my readers. I appreciate your patience.

I want to thank Dreamspinner for investing in this story, and for my amazing editing team. A big thanks for untangling and helping me polish my words.

Big shout-out and many thanks to Katie Obbink, Corvus Alyse, Danny, Desi Chapman of Blue Ink, and Litsa for listening to my dramas.

Many thanks to Sara Miller, who shared her information and experiences about the glorious and not-so-glorious details about K-pop idols.

Thanks to my friends in Japan who helped me verify what I thought I knew and explained to me what I didn't.

As always, love to my husband, who is everything to me. He was the one who decided we should go to Japan so I could visit places from *Yuri!!! On Ice*. We timed the trip in order to attend the Penis Festival. He was an incredible playmate on this fantastic trip, and he continues to be so in life.

Much love and many hugs to all.

Prologue

SAGE PULLED the elastic band off the top of his head as he paced across his makeshift vlogging cave. Now that his bleached-blond strands were free, they fell annoyingly around his face and into his eyes, but analytics showed his fans liked his chin-length hair down.

Once seated in the chair, he called up the Nakamura family game face his parents had taught him, ensured his dangling earrings hung straight, and started the camera.

"Hey, voiders. It's Sage Nakamura. Welcome to *Scream Into the Void*. Are you ready to hear me holler?"

Pointing to where the buttons would be when he placed them on the lower part of the video screen, he reminded viewers, "Like, subscribe, comment, blow me—you know the routine. I'm positive this video will get some of you angry at me, just like when I highlighted the darker side of K-pop and the painful grooming of young would-be idols. I'll link those videos in the comment section so you can relive your fury."

He shrugged. "Today's topic has nothing to do with drumming… directly. I'm just a studio drummer who is going on a bit of a rant. Your warning is the channel's name: screaming is my brand."

Grinning, Sage wiped his thumb over his lower lip and made his eyebrow arch in the way his haters called arrogant but his fans called sexy. "In the past couple of years, we've seen idols taking their own lives, fan-fiction sites being shut down in China, actors' and singers' careers being put in jeopardy, and bands in Japan imploding based on the hint of same-sex attraction."

Staring into the camera, he begged his audience's patience. "Why, you ask? People who aren't conforming to the 'don't-be-different policy' are cast out."

He snatched a drumstick and began to spin the wood between his fingers. The motion didn't provide the calm he'd hoped for, but he continued giving the camera side-eye. "I get it. We've all ingested plenty of homophobia and transphobia, making it hard for people to see being on the rainbow as anything other than terrible, sinful, against society—interject your own negative here."

Sage tried not to rock back and forth in his chair, pretending he wasn't still mortified by the bullshit he had once accepted. He twirled the wood through his fingers as if he believed if he could just spin fast enough, he could go back in time.

"Look, even with supportive parents, when I realized I was gay, it wasn't easy to admit, because I had internalized all the negative nonsense society feeds us. It took a minute before I could be honest about who I was. I had to parse through the stupid so I could get to me."

He forced his drumstick into a gentler twirl and took a big breath. Releasing the air slowly he said, "Fans are people, so they aren't immune to seeing the negative heaped onto the rainbow spectrum and putting it on the artists. But fans have the power to make or break an idol, and when sponsorship is the end-all, they have even more control."

Sage took a sip of whatever was in the cup next to him. Ew! Mistake! But he managed to swallow without making a face. "However, when such a powerful group refuses to be open to artists, idols, and performers who might be gay, lesbian, bisexual, or trans, they limit who gets seen.

"Therefore a performer needs to conform or risk ending their career. These limits deny full representation. And if we chase away nonconforming artists, how do we have any LGBT+ visibility?" His voice rose against his will, but this wasn't right.

Pull yourself together. Stay on point.

Anger wound its way through him, making his entire body coil tight. He squeezed the unbending wood of the drumstick to help him find the words. "And yes, I realize this bullshit still happens in the music/movie industry all the time, along with mistreatment of child stars and a lot of other fuckery in every industry. It happens everywhere."

Stick with the note cards! Screw the what about-ers!

Anger swirled through him—snap! The drumstick was now in two pieces. He shrugged but continued to hold the broken pieces as if his audience wouldn't notice. "But I can't help thinking if we could just widen the crack and allow LGBT visibility, it might give others a bit more breathing room. Understanding can lead to acceptance." He sighed. "I acknowledge that sounds a lot like I have a savior complex, but honestly, I just want to stop losing artists, idols, and bands I love."

Sage toyed with his earrings, making them click together. "I've done videos about bands who kick out members for even the possibility of being gay or bisexual, all over the globe. I'll add the links in the comment section. It has been, what now, six months since that's happened? But it still eats me, along with all the homophobia. Are we still in the Dark Ages?"

Thrusting out his chin, he glared at the camera. "Oh, I see. It's okay to be on the rainbow spectrum but shut the fuck up about it? That's some Clinton-era 'Don't Ask, Don't Tell' fuckery."

Sage added to the snark by cupping his ear for the next part. "Oh, I can hear Yaoihater 69 and FrogMan for Life telling me to mind my place. Well, as a gay man, where exactly is that? In LA, that's everywhere. But even in the USA, there are many places where people are killed for walking down the street holding hands with their partner or for living as their authentic selves. And in way too many countries, people can be executed for being queer."

He tossed the broken drumstick on the desk as he rambled about his grandmother from Kyoto, who warned him the nail that sticks out gets hammered down. She definitely saw him and his bleached-blond hair as being different.

Sage continued to rant. "Look, I'm not against any country's long-standing culture of conformity. Coming together as one voice and one people, you can get a lot done. I mean, you do you, but when that concept is applied to the LGBTQ community, it can have a very negative impact. Being different bears a stigma anywhere you live, and that can make coming out difficult. People on the rainbow need to see representation. Just knowing queer people exist gives hope."

He gripped his desk in an effort to keep his voice even.

"Again, the US has a fuckton of problems in this arena, but there are counterarguments to the hate. There's at least some outreach so kids know they aren't alone… the It Gets Better Project is at least a bit of hope." Damn if he didn't sound like a self-righteous prick.

Sitting back in his chair, he combed his fingers through the ends of his hair and pulled. "You've heard me before on the subject, but yeah, I'm still resenting that my two favorite rival J-pop bands—Fire and WTZ—imploded over this nonsense. So what if Watanabe Wayuu said Suzuki Zen was hot? He is. They both are, but the admission destroyed two talented bands and wiped out careers. Are you kidding me?

"I know there's next to no LGBTQIA visibility in bands. America and Europe aren't setting the bar very high either. We've only got a handful of people out, though I hope the trend is pushing the industry in a more accepting direction."

He got quiet and then articulated his point. "I'm just asking labels, fans, and bands to take a beat. I don't care if you're from the US, Asia, Europe, the Middle East, or freaking Antarctica. I'm asking you to remember that some singers, musicians, dancers, idols are kissed by the rainbow. They shouldn't have to hide who they are… and that shouldn't be the only thing that defines them. Rainbowness doesn't have to be a big deal."

On and on he flapped his lips. Maybe his points were good; maybe he'd delete the entire vlog. Didn't matter. He'd needed to purge the anger from his system. Speaking out was the only thing he could do… right?

Chapter 1

IKEDA DAIKI tugged his fox hat down on his head. Shutting the window, he hoped to block out the noise of Tokyo waking up.

He stared at the sketch pad. The first character he ever drew—his nameless love—smiled back at him in a way that still turned him inside out. Daiki had been drawing him since he was twelve years old.

No one else had ever laid eyes on him. He was Daiki's precious secret. Daiki had a treasure trove of pages and pads filled with sketches, all for himself.

The bookcases that lined one wall of the main space of his apartment were filled with the creations he shared with the world—mangas, from his one-offs to his series to his weekly serials—all neat and tidy on the shelves.

He had turned his living room and dining room into a working manga studio that fit him and his four assistants. Daiki was living his artist fantasy. All the things he'd ever wanted had come to pass.

Gently, he traced his finger over the lines that depicted the character's sexy half smile, the one that haunted his dreams... well, haunted almost everything.

If only he could chase away the loneliness with someone a little more three-dimensional, but deadlines gave him little time or opportunity to meet anyone.

His cell phone buzzed, reminding him his assistants would be here in another two hours.

Daiki needed to put away his special one, but doing so was always hard. Easing himself past the loss, he flipped through one of the sketchbooks. He hesitated on the picture of him holding his beloved tight.

The background of the sketch was a simple black sky with a huge moon. They hugged on the roof while looking at the stars. He caressed the dark hair made by his pencils as he imagined they were talking about the future and what plans they wanted to make. All the big things, like where they would live or what vacations they would take, and the small things too, like what to have for dinner.

To share his life with someone….

He flipped through the pages, drawing after drawing, and he needed to stop.

"I'm Pygmalion," he mused, tracing a finger once more over the full lips he'd drawn. He must be crazy to have fallen in love with a picture based on someone who didn't exist.

It probably wasn't healthy, but like many twentysomethings, he hadn't found his special someone… outside of two dimensions. To get to where he was in his career, he'd needed to stay laser-focused, so dating wasn't drawn into his storyboard. Though even the people he did meet, no one could compare—maybe he didn't want them to.

Letting his finger follow the gentle wave of the image's hair, he imagined this man would be smart, kind, and eager to change the world. Help Daiki explore things he'd only drawn, things like—

Work!

He gathered his drawing supplies and put them all away, then slipped the sketch pad back into the locked fireproof drawer of his desk on top of over thirty would-be mangas.

Switching to digital mode, he turned on his computer and morphed from fantasy to real life—make that as real as a *mangaka* could get.

The first of his four assistants walked in. Kobayashi Hikari was always early. She bowed and greeted him, "Good morning, Sensei," then disappeared into the second bedroom. He had designed the room for his assistants. There were bunk beds for napping or late nights, privacy to change clothing, and a closet to store their things.

She reappeared in a ninja costume.

"Morning." Since Daiki wore his fox hat to work, he could hardly criticize anyone else's method for sinking into their artistic zone.

"Who are you working on?" she asked.

"Hironori."

"Oh, I love him. I'm partial to the enemies-to-lovers trope anyway. Tie that in with a big boss falling in love with the head of a rival company… I'm all in." Her soft tone suggested she was smitten completely. His character certainly lived up to his name, which meant "benevolent ruler." Daiki had leaned into that in last month's manga.

Daiki chuckled. He couldn't deny his wish to be more like this character. Taking what he wanted in business and having no problem demanding more in love.

Hikari sighed. "You've got to love Hironori's bold ways and determination that always gets him what he wants. Though this month it looks like *who* he wants."

Brave Hironori accepted who he was, took risks, and was never lonely. "He does. You want to—"

"Yes, please." She jumped at any chance to work on this manga.

"It's just the dialogue." He needed to work on delegating, but it was hard for him not to do everything.

Hikari laughed and made grabby hands, so he sent her the files.

He scrolled through the storyboards on the screen and started to work on his edits.

His assistant Ito Rei, who seemed to have no interest in anything other than drawing, strolled in with Takahashi Ichiro, a new graduate who wanted to burn down the manga world one storyboard at a time. Sounded like they were still debating *sekkusu-banare.*

"But sekkusu-banare literally means drifting away from sex, so if that happens—" Rei interrupted herself to greet them. "Morning, Sensei. Hikari."

Ichiro followed suit and then trailed after Rei. "But how can the impact be negative on manga?"

"Later." Rei rushed to her seat and started to work.

Sighing, Ichiro gave Rei a pointed stare, but she ignored him, so he sat down.

"Greetings, Sensei. I picked up tea and soda." Last to arrive was Sato Akihiro, Daiki's high school pal, who usually worked far into the night. He should have his own studio, but their friendship caused neither to discuss it.

"Morning, Akihiro. Thank you. I forgot." Thankfully, one of Daiki's assistants always remembered.

"No problem, Sensei." Akihiro gave him a nod before ducking into the assistants' room.

Hikari popped up from behind her monitor. "I'll set up a delivery with the market down the street so the staples Sensei generously keeps on hand for us will arrive on Wednesday afternoons. Everyone get your lists to me after lunch."

"Sounds great." Less time on the day-to-day and more time to focus on drawing. His assistants really were outstanding.

Wearing his favorite maid's costume from Daiki's first spy manga series, Akihiro took his seat. He said her character was powerful and understated, exactly the way he wanted to draw, conveying much with little.

Glancing at the schedule, Daiki reminded the group, "We still have twelve days before the *ne-mu* is due on the monthly series, but it's Tuesday, so the final sketches are due on the weekly serials."

"Yes, Sensei," they each muttered.

Luckily, he didn't cut things close. He had storylines and rough sketches months in advance, and in some cases years. Whole series were just waiting for an editor's markups and a publisher's go-ahead.

He had two editors with different publishers catering to his distinctive brands and vastly unique audiences. The editors knew of each other and of his immense catalogue of unseen work that, unless he died an untimely death, he would bring forward at a slow but consistent pace. To flood the readership would overfeed them and then leave them wanting. Plus Daiki liked to imagine having time off. If he had something to do with free time, he might actually take it.

Drawing had always been his go-to. Even back when he was living with his grandfather in Inari. His grandfather ran one of the souvenir tea shops, so growing up meant every Monday began before dawn. He helped haul the supplies up the mountain, and then he'd run down the steps to get to school on time. When Daiki was old enough, his grandfather would usually stay the week. Daiki had been lonely until he found drawing and an entire world opened to him.

He adjusted his fox hat to cover his ears and allowed himself to sink deeper into the storyboards.

Beep! Beep! Beep!

It couldn't be time already. How was that possible? The day had flown by.

Daiki stopped the alarm and gathered his things. "I'm off to meet with the editor. Tonight at dinner, please order without me."

"Don't forget this." Akihiro rushed to the door, and handed Daiki his brand-new electronic drawing pad.

Daiki slipped the device into his messenger bag, next to other drawing supplies. "The train ride would have been long without a drawing app on a screen larger than my phone. Thank you."

When Daiki caught the train, the car wasn't crowded, so he sat down. He had made this trip many times over the last decade, but what if the publisher was meeting to tell him they were cancelling his series? Storyboards of how the event would play out flashed before him. The end scene was him leaving the meeting and walking home in the rain.

Then before he wrote *The End*, an imaginary Hironori leaned against the wall of his mental storyboard. His dialogue bubble said, "Let them. There's a ton of other publishers and editors who want you."

In the next story window, Hironori took a long drag on a cigarette. The cut of his chin was a bit too sharp, but the cigarette dangling from his lips gave the image a hazy sexual look. Lower on the page, Daiki envisioned Hironori staring at him. The dialogue bubble said, "Business is business. Your mangas sell." The final picture read, "But check your investment and savings accounts."

He shook himself. His life was not a manga, but somehow that's how he saw it… and someone else was drawing his story.

The train arrived at the station. As he passed the station restaurants and food shops, his stomach growled. Did he forget to have lunch? He turned at the newspaper stand and zigzagged up the steps to the street level, avoiding people.

The bustling road was filled with people hurrying home from their long day.

Daiki made the quick trip down the street, past the shopping center and an office building. He ducked his head as he entered a restaurant, then headed straight to the back room where the editor held her meetings. The only thing that changed was the prices on the menu. Now that he was a brand, each of his publishers treated him to nicer meals when they met.

"Nice to see you," he greeted her.

Saito Azami, who liked cats more than people, welcomed him with her attempt at a friendly smile. "And you."

He acknowledged her assistant, who gestured to the far chair. "Please."

After sliding past both of them to get around the table, he sat down. He'd had hundreds of these meetings over the last decade, but each time worry skittered through him.

After they ate, Azami-san held out her hand. "Let's see this week's work."

He pulled out his final sketches.

She skimmed through the pages with her red pen and gave him a few comments. Her assistant took a pass and asked a question or two. The editing ended with him having about an hour of additional work to do.

When he didn't move to leave, she asked, "Is there something else?"

"Yes. We've talked before about the direction I want to take."

Her quiet sigh indicated her frustration at his insistence. "It's almost the start of the new year."

Not for weeks, but he couldn't give up on this. "All the more reason to clear the slate. I want to move away from outdated tropes. Drawing past the titillation of a gay romance to what it means to be gay in Japan. I want to use my stories to give validation and visibility to those who need it."

She stood. "Give me some time. Let me see what's out there."

Standing, he gave her a more formal goodbye than usual or necessary.

It had started to drizzle, but at least the air wasn't cold enough to turn the sidewalks into ice. He tightened his scarf and meandered back through the crowds and neon.

Should he have been firmer? No, he'd been clear, and she did say she'd look for something. That wasn't a guarantee, but this exchange was the furthest he'd gone.

On the way to the train, he passed a semicrowded bar. People were smiling and laughing; he was tempted to stop in. Maybe he could…. But his assistants were waiting for him.

He hurried to enter the station and jogged down the stairs to the underground.

Chapter 2

WANT VISITORS? Sage got a text from the twins.

After editing his video, he was ready for a break, so he typed, *Yeah. Buzz us up.*

Ryley Griffin—or Lee as they liked to be called—and Ryder Cage, aka the twins, were already outside. The twins, so nicknamed in high school because they were always together, had decided Sage was their best friend back in ninth grade, and he didn't disagree.

Sage opened the door. With Lee in his leather skirt and band shirt and Ryder in their layers of black lace, they were polar opposites today, but they always fit together. "Lee, he/him pronouns today?"

"Well done, buddy. How did you know my pronouns are maleish today? My skirt or my lack of shaving?" Lee was gender fluid, and their pronouns changed with their presentation.

Sage rolled his eyes. "Combination."

Ryder glided across Sage's living room—slash bedroom slash dining room slash anything else he needed to live—and eased onto the sofa like the model they were and with far too much grace for the tiny apartment. Ryder was nonbinary and used them/they, though he/him pronouns didn't bother them. "As much love as I have for you, Lee, your adherence to the binary to counter the binary doesn't earn you points."

Elbowing Lee, Sage added, "Or blowjobs."

Lee simply shrugged and sighed.

"When are you going to move out of this place?" Ryder folded the sheets Sage had left rumpled under the cushions.

"What? I love my place." He'd moved in right after high school. The microapartment wasn't fancy, but the place was clean and safe.

"You sleep on the sofa," Ryder pointed out the obvious.

"Because I turned the bedroom into my work studio." Sage often repeated himself on this topic.

"It's not like you couldn't afford something with a second bedroom." Ryder grimaced and scratched at a stain on the sofa's armrest.

"You sound like my mother. I have what I need. I'm comfortable." Sage didn't want uber luxe to be comfortable. His apartment was what he as a studio drummer could afford, and he was good with that. It wasn't that Sage had been untouched by the wealth and privilege he'd grown up with; he acknowledged his head start in life. But he wanted to make it on his own.

Lee shrugged and plopped down next to Ryder, who fussed with Lee's leather skirt until it lay properly. "Are you done with your latest video?"

Frowning, Sage admitted, "Yeah. Still have to edit it, though."

Ryder grinned. "What's the topic?"

"Visibility or lack thereof."

"Again…? Seems like you have a theme going. What is this, the third in as many weeks?" Lee pointed out the obvious.

Sage paced from the galley kitchen to his favorite chair and crashed into the softness. "Fourth, but who is counting?"

"Look, had you not raised the issue, we wouldn't have known how tenuous the situation can be for gay/queer idols in Asia, or anywhere for that matter." Ryder gave Sage's knee a squeeze.

Sage sighed. "There's still so much to say about how being queer shouldn't limit what you're able to accomplish in your career. Your band shouldn't dissolve like sugar in water just because someone is brave enough to be themselves."

"Amen," Ryder said without irony.

Lee gave him a nod. "Preach."

Sage couldn't stop himself. "Something needs to be done about this. I don't have all the answers, but wouldn't it be exceptional to see some openly queer people in a band and not have the labels ditch them? Having their fans stand by them and support them? This isn't an Asian issue, a music issue, a writing issue, or even a gay issue. It's a human issue. We all deserve respect."

"Yup, we do." Ryder smiled at him.

"The first step is visibility. Seeing and understanding leads to acceptance. I want to see real musicians with more talent than looks giving me music and lyrics from their very soul. I want those people to be both on and off the rainbow. I believe the fans are ready to embrace people on various stripes of the rainbow… because they themselves might very well be on the yellow brick road."

Lee crossed his arms and turned to Sage. "So I guess you'll be putting your trust fund where your mouth is."

"Oh yes, of course he will. What should he wear?" Ryder waved the finger of judgment at him. "Certainly something better than this if you plan on being seen."

"What's wrong with jeans and a T-shirt? You told me they are fashion staples." Not that he gave a shit, but Sage was all about taking less flak from the fashionista turned model. "And wait. Why am I putting my trust fund in my mouth?"

Grinning, Lee pointed at him. "You threw down a challenge with these vlogs. Are you telling me you will not pick it up?"

"Forming a band isn't on my agenda. I live a comfortable life as a studio drummer." Sage's rock-and-roll dreams were a mere buzz in the back of his mind, one he'd shelved a long time ago.

Lee gathered up one of the stacks of books he'd piled on the coffee table. "These are new. *Music Business for Dummies*, *Music Business 101*, and why, look, all of these books appear to be about how to start a band. Imagine that."

All Sage was doing was imagining, strolling down the "would never happen but if it did" path.

Ryder reached over and felt Sage's forehead. "Are you sick? Didn't you say on your vlog there should be more bands who were open and accepting?"

"How would I—what? You two think I *could* start a band?" That was ridiculous enough to make him chuckle, but the serious expressions on their faces stopped him.

"You are a drummer." Ryder pointed to Sage's hands, which were currently twirling drumsticks.

Excitement coursed through Sage, making the sticks spin faster. No, he couldn't start a band. He tucked the drumsticks back under the cushion. "Studio drummer. Big difference from performer."

Lee shrugged. "A drummer drums."

Granted, he made a decent living off his studio gigs—and the bigger names were requesting him—but he'd never performed live.

"If you're interested, we know someone who could help make this happen." Lee was suggesting they could tap into their global network of friends.

Sage tamped down the excitement. It was a crazy risk. Besides, what did he know about starting a band—aside from a fuckton of research?

Caressing a hand down Lee's arm, Ryder asked, "Are you thinking of—"

"Who else?" Lee smirked.

Ryder strutted to the fridge and grabbed a water, showing why every designer clambered for them to be on their runway. Freezing as if a photographer had given the order, Ryder tilted their head, making their long hair slip over their shoulder, and then asked, "Would he help? We didn't exit on the best of terms."

Patting the space next to him, Lee said, "It wasn't the worst either."

Ryder rejoined Lee on the sofa.

"Who are you two talking about?" Sage needed to take back the reins of this runaway conversation.

"We know someone who could help you launch your band." They spoke in unison. It used to spook Sage when they did that, but he'd gotten used to it.

"Um, there is no band." And why did stating that fact feel wrong?

Ryder laughed. "You keep saying that, but there is. There has to be. Otherwise how do you get visibility?"

Knotting his hair on top of his head, Lee said, "Sato, from the Miszuka photoshoot I did last year, can help set you on the right path."

"Wait, didn't you two date him?" His friends had an interesting dating philosophy, and as for sex, well, no need to go into their business.

"No, his brother. Let me text him." Ryder's thumbs were flying across his phone.

Lee nodded. "It's all about creating a total platform so there's a built-in fan base to follow."

"I'm aware of how a platform works." Sage rolled his eyes. He'd had to—wait, was he really doing this?

Ryder added, "You're talking manga, anime, recording, then live shows?"

Chuckling, Sage tapped out a beat on his leg. He allowed himself to imagine his band giving validation for those who needed it. Nah. "You two are insane."

Ignoring him, Ryder continued, "Also a social media presence, commercial spots, perhaps a game show or six. Japan loves game shows. A bit of light humiliation is always a turn-on."

Lee arched an eyebrow. "Good to know."

Wait, what? Dare he ask? "Japan?"

"Where else? Both your parents are from Japan. You know the language. Why would you start your band somewhere else?"

"I have no band." How come the word "yet" was fighting to get out of his mouth?

"No, because first there should be a manga and maybe videos of the band forming." Ryder giggled and waved Sage off with purple nails.

"I'll shoot the videos, but which artist?" Lee asked as if clearing his intense photography schedule would be easy.

Sage argued, "You act like it's that simple."

Lee and Ryder studied him for a long moment. Then they shook him off like yesterday.

"Band name?" Ryder asked.

Snapping his fingers, Sage had that answer. "There's only one name for my band."

"And that is…?" Ryder asked.

"Kashi-sei. It means visibility in Japanese."

"Perfect." Giving him a kiss on either cheek, Ryder glided over to the door. "We'll come up with some artists for you to consider in a few days and start the wheels turning on all the ins and outs of starting a successful band."

Lee waved to him and followed Ryder.

How could he possibly start a band… and in Japan, no less?

Kashi-sei.

Chapter 3

"OF COURSE I can meet you there. That's on Takeshita-dōri, right?" Daiki kept his voice even, but something was up. Having two meetings in one week with an editor, and at an entirely different place, was an odd way to end this year.

"Yes, it is almost halfway down on the left-hand side," Azami-san said. "Thank you and see you there."

Daiki saved his work and put his things away. "I have an appointment. I will not make it to dinner," he told his assistants. He handed Akihiro the business credit card and avoided making eye contact. "I appreciate you for taking care of everyone."

"Of course, Sensei." Akihiro gave him a nod.

DAIKI EXITED the station and stared across the street. There was a Jumbotron displaying all the people milling down the Takeshita-dōri, and rainbow balloon art over the arch identifying the walking street.

He crossed with the group when the light turned and stepped into the wall of bodies. The slow procession down the four-hundred-meter-long street lined with shops, cafés, and photo booths could take over an hour to get to the other end.

It was a Friday afternoon, so many young people were already dressed in cosplay. No one was here to judge them, so they could show off their deepest selves.

Passing by the shop that specialized in rainbow cotton candy made him smile, and he inhaled the sweetness accented by popcorn. Growing up, he'd gotten sick on more than one of the giant rainbow spirals.

The crowd came to a standstill. He glanced up and smiled at his first manga shop, a magical place where he had discovered a world of possibilities. The thrill of holding in his hands the first BL novel he'd ever read made him smile. It had taken him thirty minutes to get the courage to purchase the story about two men in love. He had even hidden it among two other manga he found. Maybe he'd stop in on the way back to the station.

Daiki looked all around at the smiling, laughing, talking young people. They were at ease here. He too had found solace in the freedom of this street, and he wanted them to know it was okay to be different. In his daydreams, they wouldn't have to hide their need to be themselves outside of this safe space.

The crowd moved forward, and he shifted to the left, toward the restaurant. He exited the mass of people and jogged up the stairs.

As soon as he entered, Azami-san waved him over to the back corner of the empty restaurant. The tables would fill up with tourists in an hour or two, but right now she was alone. After they greeted each other, she said, "Daiki, I've got an interesting opportunity for you."

She had his attention because, unlike his other editor, she never came to him with something she didn't think would benefit them both in the long and short term.

"How would you like to work on a band manga?" she asked.

Chikushō, yes! Daiki kept his expression schooled blank. "That depends." He had learned long ago that even the greatest blessing could turn into a curse, so everything hinged on how something was given, why, and what having it meant.

Grinning, she sipped her beer. "I knew you'd say that. It's almost ground-up."

"So there's an actual band? Or it isn't formed yet?" He tamped down his excitement. No reason to think he'd be involved that deep into the process, but his editor was aware of his desire.

"No members yet. You wouldn't be included in that level, and it's an odd situation." She toyed with her napkin, not quite meeting his gaze.

"Which label?" Not that he knew many, but some he wouldn't go near just based on reputation.

"A rich kid from the States is funding the project. He's a studio drummer but seems connected." Clearly, or she wouldn't have mentioned the possibility to Daiki.

"How did you get the offer?" These didn't fall into people's laps.

"My brother's brother-in-law." She sipped some water.

Daiki vaguely recalled her referring to him once or twice. "The producer?"

"Yes. He's doing it as a favor. I anticipate he won't be all that involved, especially in the preliminary steps."

"What would you say the chances are this unformed band makes it to the music level?" Many attempting to use this step-by-step method didn't gain the audience necessary, so they never got past the manga stage.

Azami-san shrugged. "Who's to say? But this is an opportunity that would allow you to branch out into a subgenre you haven't published in yet."

True. He had several complete mangas of bands he'd drawn over the years but hadn't offered for publication. They were mostly terrible overblown storylines, but he could bend them into something interesting. "How will I find the time?"

Saito Azami never looked more like a feral cat than she did at that moment. "You'll have to cough up one or two of your hidden series. With your current staff, it'll allow you a lot of freedom to handle the extras this project will entail."

"Extras?"

"I got the distinct impression the guy who is sponsoring the band is going to need help navigating various things. As I said, he's American."

Daiki hated the idea of giving away even one of his prefinished stories. But if he wanted to do this, and he did, it meant jumping into the abyss with both feet. "Would you ease the restrictions on varying character presentation?"

"What do you mean?" she asked, as if she hadn't turned down every character idea that didn't fit into the stereotypical *uke-seme* relationship.

He kept his expression a blank mask. No sense letting her know how much this chance appealed to him. "I want to move beyond strong top and cute bottom. I have characters who have more varied interests that have been rejected each time I presented them."

"You have character control on this one and whatever you give me." Her expression said he should thank her for what took years to wrestle from her.

Daiki didn't even need words. He crossed his arms over his chest and sat back.

Azami-san sighed. "Tried and true sells."

He couldn't deny tropes sold well. "But there's a lot of variations. I want to explore the uniqueness of my characters, and I want more freedom with the storylines. I'd like to move beyond the usual BL tropes. We should be in a place where homosexuality isn't the biggest taboo, where characters take an entire series to panic over their sexuality and accept who they are only in the finale, if it ever makes it to the page."

"But there's beauty in how you present the internal struggle," Azami-san pointed out.

Daiki had long suspected she was on his side of the fence, but he'd never dreamed of asking for confirmation. "Agreed, but I want to draw about life after this struggle and look at how the characters overcome the adversity society heaps on them. I want to move beyond these outdated storylines."

Her eyes glinted. "I can tell this is a sticking point with you."

He channeled his character Hironori. "It is."

She nodded.

"Also I'm going to need a percentage, and I won't give outright licensing or the right to translation immediately." Daiki was pushing it. He'd already gotten what was most important, but he needed to be in charge of his storyboards from now on, and that included compensation.

"Agreed."

He disciplined his shock that wanted to draw him as elated.

If the band actually worked, this could be his ticket to a house in Roppongi Hills. Roppongi was an upscale residential area where many of the publishing big names had their homes. He dreamed of owning something modest with a small courtyard right in the heart.

Daiki found the infamous nightclubs in the district of Minato as appealing as they were notorious. Not that he'd ever been, but he daydreamed of going there to indulge like some of his wilder characters. Right, his fantasies of breaking with the stringent rules he kept for himself were just that, but still that's where he wanted a house.

Azami-san cleared her throat. "But you need to understand the scope of this project. It's a band, yes, but this American who is starting it has other reasons."

"Other than making money? Or playing for arenas filled with fans?"

"He's from LA… and is openly gay. He wants to be a rebellious nail."

"Ah, to purposefully stick out." That was cause to hesitate. His grandfather had warned him about being the nail that sticks out, because it will be hammered down. Every day he was reminded society would flatten him if given the chance. Anything out of the norm was often discouraged, as it might bring discord and possibly dishonor.

"Yes." The warning was in her one-word response.

"How very American of him." Daiki snorted and finished his beer. Pushing an agenda so different wasn't usual. But wasn't that exactly what he was trying to do?

Azami-san suggested, "You might consider using a different pen name."

"I've built this one." He'd built his brand with some of his most successful BL series: *College Boys*, *Workmates on Vacation*, *Tennis for Two*, *The Mob Boss Finds a Mole*, and his personal favorite, *The Artist & the Model*. To not use his carefully crafted platform didn't make sense to him.

She shrugged. "The band he's trying to create and the BL you'd be drawing would start to turn things on its head. It might even do well in the American yaoi market."

He was aware that the West used *yaoi* for the overall genre of boys' love, BL, and not just the type of story the term originally referred to. The English usage of *yaoi* came from the Japanese words for no climax, no point, no meaning. If this man was trying to make gay relationships count, to what extent, and how much was the American willing to risk to give meaning?

Leaning in, she stared him down. "Be warned, your fans might not like it."

He'd like to have the luxury to say it didn't matter, but one glance at his editor and he was reminded of all the people who depended upon his success. His failure could result in the loss of many people's jobs. "I can sell it to them."

"Are you expecting to expand your fan base with this series?" The skepticism in her voice told him she didn't see that happening.

"No, but I'm going to expand my fans' outlook." He wondered if she truly understood where this direction led.

Giving him a nod, she said, "I think careful presentation of changes in direction can get their early buy-in."

Another round of beers arrived before he could ask how slight.

They shared a look. The two of them loved art, manga, and BL and were well aware of the subtle shift taking place. But this would be sharpening the edge his work balanced on. This was standing out and straightening up for something that mattered.

She sipped her beer. "Think on it and get back to me next week."

"I will. Thank you for the opportunity." He finished his glass in silence, said his goodbye, and exited.

BEING FEARLESS was easy on Takeshita Street.

Standing on his roof, Daiki stared at the moon, though he might as well have been on a precipice. Did he have the nerve to step off into the unknown, where he might be seen and possibly exposed? Literal, much?

What would Hironori do? He would grab the opportunity with both hands and be good with whatever came from the experience.

Sato Akihiro joined him and stood in silence alongside him. He had changed out of his cosplay and didn't speak. He could go without doing so the entire night.

But just being in the same space reinforced what Daiki needed to do. This would be either the worst or best decision he'd ever made. Time would show which side the sketch landed on. Doing this was a leap of faith… something he'd never quite been able to do.

It was time to take over drawing his own life's storyboards.

He'd have to keep his eyes open and jump, hoping for the best. Daiki explained the offer and all the risk it might entail. "I've decided I will begin this new series, and I'm going to rely on you a bit more to carry on with the day-to-day. Your pay will reflect the added responsibilities."

"Yes, Sensei. How are you feeling?" Even though they had been friends for years, when they spoke of the business of their art, Akihiro was very respectful. He always called Daiki Sensei. Daiki assumed he did so to remind them both that while they were friends, their great working relationship needed to come first.

"I'm hopeful it'll turn into something that counts."

Akihiro stared at him a very long time before his lips turned up just a little in the corners. "Thank you, Sensei."

Daiki was pretty sure the thanks wasn't about the extra pay.

Chapter 4

Two months later….

SAGE'S CELL kept buzzing. He reached for his nightstand and hit the wall. What the—where was he?

He glanced around his temporary apartment. Oh, right. If he had thought his apartment in LA was small, compared to Tokyo it was expansive.

He located his phone on the shelf above the headboard and scrolled through messages from the twins checking on him.

Argh! You woke me! Sage growled as he texted Ryder and Lee.

You can't sleep all day! Lee responded.

Are you ready for your meeting? It's only a couple days away. Ryder was probably doing six things along with checking their calendar… and apparently, Sage's.

Yes.

You've been there three days. Go look around. Lee never believed in wasting time with sleep.

It's cold here. Hopefully, since it was the end of February, spring would be sprung early. His California blood was too thin.

Sunlight will help fight jetlag. Ryder had a point.

I unpacked yesterday. Today I'll get some basics. Later. That should count for something.

The past two months had been a surreal whirlwind. He had always prided himself on doing things without assistance, but with Kashi-sei, he needed help.

He'd let his parents and the twins tug on as many strings as possible to help him get this together. They got him meetings and conference calls with the right people, and after two months he believed the band might really happen.

Though Kashi-sei was no longer just a band—it had morphed into a multitiered visibility project. Bands were businesses, but Kashi-sei felt much bigger. Although that didn't relieve him of the pressure that a lot of people's livelihoods would depend on Kashi-sei's success.

Right now there were so many moving parts, and each needed guidance and attention. He let his head crash back onto the pillow.

What he needed was to find someone interested in partnering with him. Someone to bounce ideas off of and make suggestions that pushed Kashi-sei forward.

Maybe there was a manager or someone....

TWO DAYS later, Sage entered a large office building on the outskirts of Ginza.

His first face-to-face was scheduled to begin. Nakamura smile on, he adjusted his tie, which felt more like a noose.

He approached the receptionist precisely at 9:59 a.m. He bowed. "My name is Sage Nakamura. I have a meeting with—"

She bowed. "Allow me to take your coat."

Once she handed his coat off to someone, she said, "Right this way, sir," and led him down a hallway, opened the door, and bowed again.

He stepped inside the corner conference room, which had a long black table topped with bottles of water, teacups, tea, and wrapped treats. Two of the walls were all-glass windows overlooking Tokyo. There was a whiteboard in the corner, a huge monitor, and several computers scattered throughout the room.

A teacup shattering into pieces echoed around the room, drawing his attention to the man at the other end of the table.

The man muttered his apologies in Japanese but kept his intense gaze on Sage, making him feel like he was being inhaled.

Who was he? The man wore a navy suit, but instead of a button-down and a tie, a graphic T-shirt with some colorful anime characters peeked out from his jacket. The cut of the suit highlighted the man's height and his broad shoulders. Sage couldn't help but wonder how he looked from the back.

Other people quickly cleared up the mess, but Sage couldn't rip his gaze from the other man's.

A woman in a dark suit approached him.

Sage forced himself out of his bemusement. He pulled the business-card holder his mother had given him out of his suit pocket and held it in his left hand.

"I'm Saito Azami from BL Delight. We spoke on the phone." They bowed to each other and exchanged cards.

"I'm Sage Nakamura, founder of Kashi-sei."

He accepted her card in his left hand and placed it on his business-card holder as he handed her his card so the writing faced her. Taking a moment, he studied her card.

Don't shake hands unless she reaches out. "I'm very pleased to meet you in person, Saito-san. Please call me Sage."

Saito Azami reached out and shook his hand. "Call me Azami."

The familiarity was a bit surprising, but during his father's drill sessions on business etiquette, he had warned Sage that some people would try to put him at ease by adopting some Western customs. He needed to just go with it. In the US some of his family expected traditional Japanese manners while others wanted American culture only, so skipping back and forth felt normal to him. Though he'd be mindful of what the norm in Japan was, he'd take people at their word and respect their lead.

"May I present our renowned mangaka, Sensei Ikeda Daiki," Azami continued. As the man who'd murdered the teacup stepped over and bowed, Sage couldn't help but notice how attractive he was.

His elegant face was accented with high cheekbones. He had a wide, generous mouth that made Sage think of the many things he'd like to do with it—the most urgent of which was to taste those lips. *Stop!*

Wait, mangaka? He's the artist? The twins had said BL artists were mostly women. Sage had assumed the artist's male name had been chosen for privacy.

But no, Sensei Ikeda Daiki was an incredible artist… and very male.

Sage's smile faltered, but he dropped into a bow, hopefully covering his shock.

"Please call me Daiki." The man held out a beautiful hand—long fingers with impeccably manicured nails—to Sage.

"I'm Sage." A nice firm handshake, but Daiki's hands were soft and warm.

Sage started to get lost in Daiki's lovely deep brown eyes. Flecks of amber reflected in their depths like a faceted jewel. Sage dropped his eye contact; he didn't want to be seen as too aggressive. Damn, being attracted to someone shouldn't mean he lost all semblance of etiquette.

Then he looked down. Had he ever been this affected? Oh shit! Business card....

Sage took the offered business card with two hands, studied the graphics. The logo was a tiny sketch pad with a man's face on it and pencils scattered around it. He wanted to get a closer look, but a magnifying glass would be necessary, so he put the card with Azami's on top of his business-card holder. He presented his own card with two hands as well.

Daiki's fingers grazed his, and Sage's entire body went on alert. Maybe he should have gotten laid before moving here, but he'd been so busy that even a Grindr hookup seemed like too much work.

Azami introduced her two assistants.

He forced his attention on the two people. They exchanged bows and business cards.

Then Azami gestured to the seat at the head of the table. "I suggest we begin."

Everyone stood by their seats.

His father had drilled into him the importance of seating around a table. The ancient tradition still held. The honored top seat, or *kamiza*, was farthest from the door and was meant to be his. The *shimoza*, or lowest seat, was the one closest to the door—because that's who would be killed first. Not that they were expecting an invasion.

Expectation rode him, but sometimes he couldn't help if his American roots showed up. Time to begin as he planned to move forward.

Smiling at Daiki, he gestured to the head of the table. "Please, Sensei."

Daiki gave him the smallest of grins before he slid a second seat to the head of the table and eased into it, garnering a surprised look from the editor and her assistants, which he appeared not to notice. He gestured to the other seat. "Please, Sage." The way his name sounded on his lips.... "It's Daiki."

Sage grinned at him.

Oh, well done! All his adult life he'd been looking for someone who not only would enjoy the candy he gave but also give some in return!

No one said anything, but he wondered if any of them remembered that one of the big bosses in Daiki's *Workmates on Vacation* did the same thing for a rival to signal his interest. The rival countered by adding a chair because he was okay being equal to the man but not over him. Not that Sage was signaling his… *oh, double damn him to hell.*

He carefully stacked the business cards on top of his card holder and set the pile in front of him.

Azami started. "BL Delight appreciates you choosing to work with us on this endeavor. All the legal agreements are signed. Why don't we discuss a schedule to proceed?"

Sage nodded and glanced around at the people sitting at the table, but Ikeda Daiki—Daiki—was where his attention drifted again and again. Sage shifted his body to pick up subtle nonverbal cues as Daiki sketched across the page. A faceless band emerged from the empty whiteness.

Daiki turned his head and saw Sage watching him. His pencil froze, and he set it down. "My apologies."

Azami cleared her throat. "Sensei, BL Delight understands and appreciates your need to sketch the details around you, but Mr. Nakamura might not—"

"It's Sage—and Daiki, please continue. I don't see your drawing as disrespect but as reinforcing my faith in you." Plus Sage wanted to see what would emerge from the page under Daiki's attention.

"Thank you for understanding." Daiki nodded but didn't look at Sage. He flipped his pad of paper over, but he still held the pencil.

Azami went through the basic timeline from the release of the first manga to ten months for the anime, with recording and concerts falling into place after that. Then she started to dial down on how they would accomplish each step. "Of course, that's only the typical schedule. Kashi-sei's might be different. You'd be better equipped to marry the music schedule needed to meet the timeline, so I will leave that to you. However, we've engaged an agency to review and select the candidates for the other band members and—"

Daiki's grip on his pencil tightened.

"You don't agree, Daiki?" Sage couldn't help but ask.

"It's not my place to disagree on anything other than my manga, and since that's not being discussed, I have no need to say anything," Daiki stated without emotion.

Wow, Sage's dad would have been impressed by how the noncommittal statement completely sank any option of moving forward without exploring what he meant. "Except who the band members are does affect the manga and... what?"

Daiki's eyes widened as if he'd been surprised that Sage caught he wanted to say more. "I've learned to keep my storylines and sketches general enough to please but retaining the ability to change direction as needed."

Sage cocked his head and stared at Daiki. When Daiki's gaze met his, Sage's heart tripped over itself, and it was as if he were being caressed and stroked in all the right places. Daiki bit his lip and looked away, and Sage wanted to get his attention back.

Azami cleared her throat, reminding Sage other people were in the room.

Daiki glanced back at him.

This might be crazy, but their connection was total and immediate, and his dad had taught him to go with his gut. Settling back into Daiki's gaze, Sage stated, "It would be better if you were involved in every step of the process."

Daiki gave a sharp inhale. His eyes screamed yes, but he said, "That's not usually done."

Azami shook her head. "No, it is not."

Her words snapped into sharp focus for Sage. He didn't care. "In other ventures that's probably true. Maybe. But I want—need—involvement at a deeper level."

His dad's wisdom echoed in his head, reminding him that Daiki had gotten a great deal in terms of percentage points beyond the manga, so he'd definitely be vested in the band's success. Could Daiki be a real partner in this?

"What do you say, Daiki?"

Daiki's long eyelashes fluttered for a moment, and his lips curled up ever so slightly. "Let's see how matters proceed."

Those words felt like everything to Sage. A start. A win. A completion. "What would you recommend?"

Raking his fingers through his shoulder-length hair, Daiki said, "You should be choosing the members. A talent agency won't have all of the factors you wish to consider as their filter. If I understand, your intention is visibility. They might not be filtering based on your hopes. I imagine you'd know what to look for in the members better than anyone else."

Sage had assumed the agency would know best, and even if he could work with anyone, having more control would be better. But what did he know about interviewing people?

"Would you have time to interview with me?" Sage pushed the boundaries, but that's what this was about.... Okay, this had nothing to do with the greater good. Hopes of convincing Daiki to be more of a partner and, well, possibly wanting to spend more time with Daiki factored into the suggestion.

Azami shook her head. "Oh, Sage, I'm sorry. I don't think Daiki would have the time with all his deadlines."

She was either trying to give him an out or didn't want Daiki involved to that level.

Daiki's frown turned into a smile as he addressed Azami. "I appreciate you trying to respect my time and manage me, but I would like to accommodate Sage's request."

Sage got the distinct feeling he was stepping in it. "She's probably correct. You're too busy to—"

Pressing his lips together for a moment, Daiki took a deep breath and released it. His eyes narrowed. "I'd like to help you. Boys' love, or yaoi, as you call the genre in the West, is meant to have no climax, no point, and no meaning. As my editor knows, I want to change that, and working with Kashi-sei will give more purpose to my work."

"Your work has touched so many people already." Sage wanted Daiki to know that.

Daiki tilted his head and shifted closer, allowing Sage to inhale a rare treat. Daiki's light scent wasn't overwhelmed by hair product, and an earthy patchouli mixed with a subtle hint of jasmine set Sage's imagination on fire.

"You know my work?"

"I've read a few of your series," Sage admitted. Though he'd stop the confession there, otherwise he'd begin gushing about how hot the characters were, and how the interesting and sexy storylines kept him up in more than one way.

Daiki looked away from Sage's gaze and then said, "I'd like to be more direct with some points and have them make more of an impact."

"Yes. Exactly." Excitement wound through Sage. Everyone else around the table disappeared, and the moment hung between them.

Finally, after endless phone calls and emails exchanged with various people organizing this project, Sage felt someone was buying into what he wanted to do, not just giving him lip service.

"If I may interject." Azami leaned forward, gaining their attention. "The agency has already set up interviews for next week, starting on Tuesday. Why don't you scan the list and insert yourself into the process that is already set up? It will save you time. I can make the call arranging this… if you'd like."

Sage looked at Daiki, who inclined his head. "Yes, we'd appreciate that."

Azami stood. "I'll email you the specifics."

After a quick round of goodbyes, he was left with Daiki. They stared at each other for a long moment and then sat back down.

Wondering out loud, Sage asked, "So what is your process?"

Daiki traced his fingers over the pad in front of him as if he were still sketching. "Once the choices are made, you and the bandmates will most likely live together."

Hmm, living together. "Right, I'd be living with several strangers to collaborate."

"Forgot about the livestreams, TikToks, and YouTube videos necessary?" Daiki set down his pencil and poured Sage some tea.

Such a simple act, but not one of the guys Sage had dated—not even the two longer-term boyfriends he'd had—had ever poured him tea.

Sage swallowed the weird emotion that threatened to surface.

This was Japan. Everyone poured for their companions, but the only ones who ever did that for him were family. The simple act shouldn't matter, but it did.

Why was he getting up in his head?

Sage gave Daiki a nod and then filled a cup of tea for Daiki with care.

Daiki received the teacup with two hands and a very sweet smile. He drank it all before setting the cup down.

Sage snapped himself back from the land of emotions and refilled the cup. "So you'll be hanging out wherever the band is?"

"Yes. I will spend as much time as possible so the manga can reinforce Kashi-sei's brand. I need to absorb who each member of the band is, and being with the band will help me find storylines."

"It makes sense." Sage liked that idea a bit too much. The twins would remind him he wasn't here to get a boyfriend but to make a difference.

Daiki twirled the pencil between his fingers. "I am hoping the manga and story arcs can be as close to reality as possible without negatively impacting you... or the other members. The themes will reinforce living your true self and visibility."

The excitement that had dissipated during the preparation for this move found Sage again and skipped through him. "It's been a whirlwind since I decided on doing this, and I haven't had much time to think about the specifics."

Daiki sipped his tea. "May I ask a question?"

"Sure." Sage refilled Daiki's cup and then slid a wrapped bun in front of Daiki and himself.

Positioning his cup with care, Daiki looked at him. "Why are you doing this?"

"I'm tired of gay equating to a problem. I want to hold up a mirror so people can see how ridiculous that is." Sage drank his tea.

Daiki refilled Sage's cup and remained silent, as if he were waiting for more.

Sage could give him more. Rage-filled years of too much, but he'd keep it simple. "Do you remember Fire and WTZ?"

"Of course. You couldn't go anywhere without being bombarded with their pictures and songs."

Sage spun the plastic-wrapped bun. "There are lots of reasons, but in LA you can be gay and not feel much, if any, negativity. I've been spoiled in many ways, but what happened to them really angered me. Watanabe Wayuu's and Suzuki Zen's bands imploded due to one hint of same-sex attraction."

Daiki stared at the table and then studied at him. "Would you consider either of them?"

Would he? "Of course, but I doubt they would.... Is there a way of asking?"

"I'll ask my editor to include that request in the email. The agency can contact their agents." Daiki typed on his phone for a few moments before giving him a nod.

If that could work…. "That would be full circle, since they are one of the original reasons I became so angry. Sometimes this whole process seems overwhelming."

Daiki nodded. "Um…. Do you have some free time?"

Was Sage being asked out? "Yes, why?"

"I'd like to take you to Animate." Daiki moved toward the door.

"Animate?" Sage followed.

Daiki grinned as they accepted their coats. "Seven floors of all heaven for fans of manga, anime, yaoi, and games. It's filled with merchandise, books, and DVDs."

After a quick train ride to Akihabara, they started hiking up the stairs toward the street level.

At the second landing of the steps, Daiki stopped and pointed behind them. "Sage, hold on. Turn around."

A huge billboard of six stunning men striking poses against a glittery background loomed in front of them. "They look familiar. A new musical group?"

Daiki nodded. "Yeah. You've probably seen one of the many pictures of them around Tokyo. Every convenience store has their faces on magazines, game cards, and special products. They are everywhere."

Sage had even seen their image at the airport. Impressive, actually. "Branding at its finest."

"Animate is just few blocks this way." Daiki directed them to the flagship store.

Slipping on his gloves, Sage braced himself for the cold as they hit street level.

Tokyo felt like a mix of New York City and downtown LA. People were moving and focused. Their path took them past bars, restaurants, stores, hotels, and apartment buildings. There was a city energy that invigorated Sage but didn't overwhelm him.

Daiki paused and grabbed a knit hat out of his messenger bag. He pulled it down over his ears and put on a pair of heavy-rimmed glasses. Once his reverse Superman was done, he gestured to a tower. "I present Animate."

Sage followed Daiki through the first floor—filled with action figures, T-shirts, cell phone dangles, and various other merch—to the elevator.

"The kids are still in school, so it's not crowded yet." Daiki indicated with a slight bow and gesture that Sage should step in the elevator first; then he pressed the top-floor button. The door closed, revealing a picture of the men from the billboard.

The doors opened to cardboard cutouts of six anime characters who looked like the guys following Sage around Tokyo. "Is this the band from the billboard?"

Daiki nodded. "Exactly. If you look around this area, you can see how they built up their audience base at each step."

Sage walked off the elevator and into what looked like an exhibition. There were pictures and write-ups of the same six guys who looked like the anime characters. A bookshelf housed all the same series of manga. Some of the TVs suspended from the ceilings and walls depicted an animated show of the characters, while others featured the six guys singing. The counter displayed music and anime DVDs of the group.

"And now they are doing concerts." Sage pointed at the poster behind the salesperson.

She smiled at him. "Tickets go on sale next weekend."

"Thanks." Sage smiled.

Her eyes narrowed in on Daiki. "You look familiar. Wait, I know—"

"Nah, I only look like him." Shaking his head, Daiki turned and headed toward the door.

Daiki didn't wait for the elevator, so Sage chased behind him down the stairs and tried not to chuckle. "An ex?"

Stopping midstep, Daiki shook his head and gave him a quick "No."

Not that it meant anything, but that put a bounce in Sage's step.

Pausing at the fourth floor, Daiki asked, "Mind if I stop for a moment?"

"Of course not."

The floor was filled with shelves of manga, novels, and art magazines.

"I haven't done this in a while. I just want to check on my titles. Usually my assistants do this, but I'm here." Daiki made a direct line to shelves on the far left.

There was a whole section of shelf space dedicated to Ikeda Daiki. Sage pointed and grabbed a book. "Hey, this is all you?"

Daiki nodded and put a finger to his lips, indicating Sage shouldn't let the world know that. The disguise made more sense now. Turning back to the shelf, Daiki ran a hand over his section. He stopped and put a book right side up, then reshelved three others in the correct order. "Thank you."

"That's it?" Sage closed the book he was trying not to drool into. They had only been there for three minutes.

"Yes." Daiki turned on his heel and nodded to the salespeople behind the counter.

Sage sighed and replaced the title he held. Maybe he'd make a trip here tomorrow. The train seemed clean and straightforward.

At the bottom of the train station steps, Daiki asked, "Do you know how to get back to your apartment?"

Pulling out his phone, Sage displayed a train app. "I don't, but this does."

Daiki smiled and shifted from foot to foot. "I am looking forward to working with you on this."

Nodding, Sage tried to think of something great to say and failed.

"Well, I should let you get on with your day." Daiki pointed in the opposite direction Sage's app suggested. "I'm heading this way."

"Oh… um, yeah. Okay." *Think of a reason to go that way….*

Daiki waved and hurried down the hallway. He stopped before getting on the down escalator and waved at Sage.

As he disappeared, Sage tried not to be bummed. Maybe he'd head back to Animate and get some of Daiki's titles… as more research. Kindle mangas were great, but there was something about holding a paperback in his hands. He headed back to Animate to spend more time in Daiki's world… or in the ones he created.

Chapter 5

ON TUESDAY, Daiki stepped off the train and was greeted by the very first signs of spring. A few of the trees had more than bare branches; on the very tips some had tiny buds of pink beginning to form. He hurried the short distance to an art deco building downtown. Today he would be sitting in on the meetings Sage Nakamura was having with the musicians.

"Ow." He flexed his right hand. Rubbing at the pain didn't take away the pleasure he'd had putting all the storyboards and ideas that had rushed to the surface on the page.

He entered the sleek conference room, and just the sight of Sage made Daiki's heart do a flip, illuminating why the last three days had also felt like years.

There was something Daiki always found alluringly rebellious about a man with bleached-blond hair. Who knew he had such a thing for hair caught up in a messy bun? Lots of teenagers wore their hair this way, and the style had never made an impact on him… until now.

What was happening? Did he think himself a character in one of his BLs? This was business, and by making this project successful, he'd get what he craved… more freedom in content and presentation. He peeked over at Sage.

His breath was stolen by how incredibly sharp and put together Sage looked in his tailored sports jacket over a graphic T-shirt. He swallowed hard as he couldn't help but notice how the tight black denim stretched over his thighs.

So what? The guy knew how to dress.

Daiki forced himself to walk slowly to greet the person from the agency, Hina Mori. After all due respect had been paid, he turned his full attention to Sage. His fingers itched to capture that smile. The way his lips curled, it was almost a smirk, but the gleam of true pleasure in his eyes kept it out of the realm of the sarcastic.

"It is good to see you, Sage." Daiki broke out his English on the off chance it might make Sage smile.

They bowed to each other.

"It's a pleasure." Sage's deep voice had an accent that made Daiki shiver.

The smile they exchanged stretched out until the door opened and the first candidate walked into the room.

Strut would be a better term. His greeting lacked respect, and his arrogance seemed directed at Sage.

Sage either didn't pick up on the disregard or chose not to respond as he went right into the concept of the band. "I want Kashi-sei to promote an understanding and acceptance of people who might be different."

"Different how?" The interruption set Daiki on edge. Who did he think—

Apparently not affected in the least, other than a tightening of his jaw, Sage explained, "Different in many ways, but mostly in terms of orientation or gender identity."

"No way. What you're proposing is career suicide." The man stood and left without even a goodbye.

Sage inhaled and dropped his head for a moment, then pasted a smile on his face. "I'm guessing there was no prescreen?"

The agent shook her head. "Not for that."

He gave a nod. "Who's next?"

AFTER A couple of days filled with interviews, a definite pattern had developed. They greeted the candidate, they sat, and Sage described the band's goal of visibility. The reactions varied, but none had been positive.

This guy shot a wide-eyed stare to his agent and then grimaced.

Sage smiled. "I think—"

The guy stood. "Well, you shouldn't. This isn't your concern, so butt out." He spoke in English, clearly calling Sage out as a Westerner and an outsider.

On cue, Daiki and Sage stood and thanked the musician for their time. No sense prolonging rejection.

Sage collapsed back into his chair and let his head hit the table. "He's right. It's not my place."

The representative from the agency organizing these meetings stared at him and Daiki for a moment. She pointed toward the door, and as soon as Daiki gave her a nod, she escaped.

"Wrong is wrong in any place or any time and in any language. Isn't that what you said?" Daiki remembered the quote because the words added fuel to his own fire.

Sage's head rolled to the side. "When did I—you've watched *Scream Into the Void*?"

"I listened to a few episodes while I was drawing over the weekend." Daiki didn't confess he'd devoured almost all of them.

"Um… still, what am I doing?" Sage's eyes crinkled up in the corners as he looked at Daiki for answers.

Many commenters on Sage's channel had encouraged him to move forward with the band. They approved of the band's name, Kashi-sei, because there was no doubt as to the brand.

Daiki repeated what many of the commenters had written to Sage. "If not you, who?"

"You. With you agreeing to be my partner in this." Sage grinned as he nodded, as if coming to some great conclusion.

Daiki straightened and focused his gaze out the window. *What do I know about anything other than drawing? This is crazy.* "I'm a mangaka."

"And an incredible one, but I've always known I couldn't do this alone. I hoped to find someone to help me drive this and bounce ideas around with—and here you are. Maybe you thought I was joking when I asked you the day I met you, but there's one thing I've learned from my dad: if you know it's right, go for it."

"I wouldn't know where to begin." Visibility and validation seemed like an unreachable goal.

"I know you've been using the power of your pen for this cause for a long time now," Sage said.

Daiki folded his arms over his chest, crushing his attempt at business wear and his magenta tie in the process. He was unsure why what Sage had said was hard to believe, since his work was quite popular. Of course Sage would have vetted his work, but the idea shouldn't please him this much. Turning away from the window, he stared at Sage. "You've said you read some of my work?"

"Yes, and I've read more since I got to Japan. I could see that you've been slowly elbowing your way into a different space with both of your publishers."

"I didn't think it was noticeable." A little personal agency here, add some validation there, and an overall lessening of stereotypes whenever he could. But he hadn't expected anyone to catch on. Most of the BL genre had been doing this gentle shift for years. Though in truth his was more pointed and had a definite purpose.

Sage raised his head from the table and grinned. "If I read your work over time, I might have missed the results, but with binge reading, I could easily see you've been driving this agenda for a while."

"Mm." Daiki didn't know what else to say, but to have someone see him shot a spark through him.

Sage's gaze traveled from his head to his toes, and on the way back up, he stopped and stared at Daiki's lap. Sage wiped his thumb across his own lips, making Daiki wish he could feel the softness of that mouth.

He wasn't used to such an open, appreciative stare. The appraisal embarrassed and excited him in equal measure. But he was drawing his own storyboard, so he glanced directly into Sage's eyes.

Their gazes locked.

His heart started beating faster, and Daiki felt like he was tumbling down but being held aloft at the same time. He couldn't resist the desire to be trapped in Sage's attention.

The storyboards were all laid out in front of his mind's eye. He painted the shy artist being enthralled with the bold foreign musician, the folly of beginning a relationship doomed to end but unable to prevent one because the more they knew of each other, the more the desire grew, and then....

Totally not on the agenda.

Snapping out of overdone BL tropes, Daiki asked, "How do you recommend we proceed?"

Sage groaned. "I haven't a fucking clue—sorry."

"No worries." Daiki enjoyed how free Sage was with his words. He'd never spent time with anyone from America, but Sage was exactly what he'd pictured an American to be—not that all Americans were like Sage, and he imagined few could live up to his fantasy. Sadly enough for him, Sage did.

Sage's head dropped.

A need to soothe him spread through Daiki like a marker pressed down and bleeding over the page. He rested a hand on Sage's shoulder, which tensed for a moment before relaxing. "What you're doing is an exceptional thing, but you knew it wouldn't be easy. It's frustrating."

Sage's head turned to the side, allowing Daiki to get a glimpse of warm brown eyes he couldn't quite fully capture, peering through the thick curtain of his hair.

Daiki tried to absorb every detail to get him on page later... or at least a reasonable copy of him. He let his hand slip away.

Pushing up on one elbow, Sage propped his head in his hand, giving Daiki another picture to sketch. "It is. I knew it wouldn't be simple, but going through this process is another matter."

"Singers and actors feel compelled to respect the power of the fans. Maybe a bit too much." Even he felt the effects of this public contract, which caused him to strain to meet his fans' needs without stressing his creativity.

Sage nodded. "We have much of the same in the US. We build stars up as mega gods and goddesses and then look for reasons to knock them off the pedestals we erected."

"Some fans feel a personal responsibility to guide a singer or actor to fame and stardom," Daiki noted. "Stars represent some products in the US, but I don't think as much as here. In Japan, and other places in Asia, fans gain status by purchasing and uploading photos with the products, tagging the star as well as their fandom."

Sighing, Sage said, "I know. That's why I thought taking the need to please sponsors and investors out of the equation would allow more freedom and might help lessen the ties to fan expectation and sponsor demand."

"Don't lose faith. There's more musicians to see."

"See, that's what I mean. You believe in this as much as I do. I need you... as a partner. Agree?"

The company rep bounced back in, filled with renewed energy. "Ready for the next candidate?"

Sage stood. "Let's do this... *partner*."

Happiness Daiki had only experienced when he'd beat all deadlines against the odds colored him in vivid contrast to the past. He didn't agree to be a partner, but he didn't say no, which Sage obviously took as a yes, and Daiki chose to leave it at that.

The afternoon sunlight picked out various shades of blue-black in the roots of Sage's hair while the bleached part glittered in shades of gold. His cheeks tinted a soft pink and his eyes sparkled whenever his gaze landed on Daiki, pushing Daiki right back into an angsty BL drama that he desperately wanted to co-star in.

His breath caught. How could he ever do justice to Sage on the storyboards? But the louder question was how could a shy mangaka ever hope to have even a small piece of an LA drummer? The story in his head played out to a hopeless ending.

What would one of his bolder, brassier characters do? Maybe if he channeled someone else—no, that would never work.

"The last candidate of the day," Sage whispered as the door opened.

A sharply dressed person with short hair, wearing a suit, appeared next to the company representative. "May I present—"

"Yamamoto Haru. Pleased to meet you." Sage was on his feet.

Daiki wasn't sure if he should use the male or female pronouns. And after they exchanged greetings, he still wasn't sure.

"I'm pleased to meet you both."

The representative slid a page containing details about the candidate's experience in front of each of them.

Sage said, "Feel free to speak Japanese, unless you'd rather continue in English."

Daiki hoped not, because while he could understand the language, he found reaching for the right words a pain.

"Thank you." Haru gave a quick nod.

Sage smiled. "My pronouns are him, he, and his. I want to double-check your pronouns are also him, he, and his."

The ease of Sage's straightforward question caused everyone else to pause.

Haru leaned back, and then a slow smile turned up their lips. "I'm not used to that question."

Sage held his hands in front of him. "I'm sorry. I don't mean to make you uncomfortable."

Haru glanced at Daiki for a moment, then stared at Sage. "Yes, he, his, and him are my pronouns… but not legally."

The reference to the 2004 law that wouldn't allow gender identity on legal documents to be changed unless the person was sterilized and had affirmation surgery couldn't be missed. Human rights advocates were working on getting that changed but to Daiki's knowledge had yet to do so.

Sage frowned and gave a slow nod. "Yeah, many states in the US have similar outdated laws. And if this works out with you and the band, what we put on pay stubs won't affect what the other band members or fans address you as."

Haru straightened his tie. "So he, him, and his, then?"

Sage didn't hesitate and launched into his speech. "Absolutely. I want everyone in Kashi-sei to be themselves. It's my hope our visibility will allow our fans to feel free to be the same way. You can be as open or closed as you want about yourself, but every member needs to be respectful of every other member and honor who they are. I want Kashi-sei to be a touchstone for people who need validation. I want them to know being LGBTQIA+ doesn't mean there's something wrong with them and that they are never alone."

Haru gripped the table with both hands and leaned in. "I'm good with all of that. But why would you want me to be part of this?"

Sage tilted his head and grinned. "I've seen you play. You come highly recommended. Why wouldn't we want you?"

"I've never been in a band before." Haru tossed that out as if it didn't matter, but he studied every move Sage made.

Daiki skimmed the information about Haru in front of him, looked up at Sage and then Haru. "But you've performed with a number of them."

Haru crossed his arms and sat back. "I have."

Glancing up from the information, Sage said, "From what I understand, you play anything with strings, and you've saved a number of bands from canceling shows by being able to step in last minute. And you've played both small venues and large arenas."

Shrugging like it was not a major feat, Haru tapped the spec sheet about Kashi-sei and the description of the band's expectations. "I've seen your channel, so I understand the basics of why you are doing this. The salary says you either think I'm really worth that or you know I could be ending my career before it starts by accepting if an offer is given."

Sage drank from the cup in front of him and then replaced it on the table with care. "I won't lie. This could all be problematic for everyone's future in the Japanese music business. There's no way around that risk other than to allow it not to be a financial burden."

Haru smiled, then schooled his expression into something more neutral. "You two are really serious about this?"

Sage nodded. "We've hired a social-media guru and a manager. My friend will be doing the video pieces of the band to arouse interest. I'm leveraging my YouTube channel and its platform. Daiki will be penning the manga, and then we'll do an anime while the band is prepping the music to perform concerts."

Haru spun the paper in front of him. "Where are the songs coming from?"

"I know some songwriters in LA…." Sage tilted his head. "Why? Do you write?"

Haru shrugged. "A bit. If we move forward, I'd like to submit some of my songs for review."

"Of course. I'd be interested in seeing whatever you'd like to share." Sage sounded excited at the prospect.

Squinting at Sage as if afraid of missing something, Haru nodded in slow motion. "Okay… and Kashi-sei is a band that plays instruments, not an idol group, right?"

Sage grinned. "Correct. Though we might change things up for a song or two, but for the most part we'll be playing music."

Haru gave a nod of acceptance seeming to accept Sage's words, then he leaned forward. "Who else are you interviewing?"

Sage glanced over at Daiki. "Should we?" was the unasked question.

Daiki inclined his head and continued to imagine drawing Haru. The problem was going to be figuring out the right angles on his hair flip and how the black liner made his eyes huge but even more masculine.

Sage smiled over at the company representative and said, "Please show him our list."

She frowned at the odd turn of events but did as requested.

Once Haru got the list, he skimmed his finger down the names. He shook his head.

"What?" Sage asked.

"First three on your list are rather useless. Next one is okay but shows up late for practice and shows. This one, she's pregnant, plans to get married and semiretire. The rest of the list is trouble but…."

"But?"

"Even with their issues, Watanabe Wayuu and Suzuki Zen are excellent singers. They both play several instruments. Watanabe Wayuu can kill it on guitar, and Suzuki Zen's fingers can set any keyboard on fire. Each has a strong fan following, but they would be chaos… together."

"Together… both of them?" Sage seemed to be mulling the idea over.

"When someone's drunken comment implodes two bands, I'd label them as chaotic trouble."

Sage's smirk should have worried Daiki, but instead it excited him and reminded him not only the singers would be trouble.

"Chaotic might be interesting." Sage smirked.

The company rep started coughing.

Haru grinned. "If you can get either or both of them, close the deal. They would add a lot."

Daiki nodded. He couldn't agree more.

HARU LEFT, promising to have someone look over the contract and requesting to sit in on the next meetings.

Sage turned to Daiki. His big smile was enough to melt Daiki like crayons left too close to a heater. He looked away to keep himself from staring.

"Thank you, Daiki. I couldn't have done that without you."

Daiki ignored the warm feeling Sage's exaggerated praise gave him. "I'm sure you could have."

Putting his hands palms out in front of him, Sage said, "Let's just say I'm glad I didn't have to. So we need to celebrate. Where do you go to celebrate?"

"Nowhere" didn't sound cool, so Daiki went with, "We normally work until late, so I usually have dinner with my assistants."

"No bars to have a few drinks? Or a club to dance?" After Daiki shook his head, Sage continued, "How about we change that?"

Daiki reached in deep and accessed the parts of himself he infused into his characters. Afraid if he opened his mouth he'd say no, he gave Sage a nod.

Sage shifted as if his energy could barely be contained. "How about Ni-chōme?"

Ni-chōme? Ni-chōme? There was no denying that was where gay men and women, along with people who were transgender, went to be themselves. Of course Sage would want to go there; he was openly gay.

Daiki scrambled to say, "I've never been to Ni-chōme."

"Oh, really. Never?" Sage studied him, making him feel like he'd failed to turn in his final drafts on time.

"I don't go out much." But somehow Daiki found courage not to leave it there. He admitted, "But I've always wanted to go there."

"Well, then, let's lose our virginities together." Sage's words rolled off his tongue and teased Daiki physically.

"Um...." Daiki swallowed hard. Was Sage making fun of his inexperience? No, Sage couldn't know that.

"Yeah, the last trip here, I was too young to drink, and my parents were with me, so this will be my first time too."

Daiki relaxed. "Sounds good."

He swallowed the addition of "Too good."

Why did I agree to meet for drinks? Daiki took a deep breath and stared out over the other rooftops in Tokyo. He had showered, changed his clothing three times, and now wanted to back out.

Akihiro joined him. "You look nice."

"I'm supposed to meet someone for drinks. I should cancel."

Akihiro had changed out of his cosplay clothing, and there was a sadness around his eyes. "Don't waste your life."

"What?" They were longtime friends, but Akihiro was always careful not to let that part of their relationship show in front of the others.

Akihiro sighed. "Take a chance on being happy, my friend."

"How do you know I'm not?" He wasn't, but he'd thought he'd been hiding it.

"You're up on the roof trying to look for a way out of going to whoever has gotten you dressed up."

"I'm not—" Akihiro's arched eyebrow stole the rest of Daiki's lie. "I will go, but what about you?"

"My time has passed. My wife is divorcing me." Akihiro laid his pain out in such a matter-of-fact way.

What could Daiki say without being intrusive? "Akihiro... I'm sorry."

"One in three marriages now end in divorce. This is not unusual. We agree it's time. Neither of us is pleased with our lives." He patted Daiki on the back. "This is why I'm telling you to live and enjoy."

Daiki couldn't help his friend or himself. "This is going to be a disaster."

"Isn't it you who reminds all of us that the best stories are?"

Chapter 6

SAGE STOOD under the Forever 21 sign, which cast a rainbow of colors onto the sidewalk. His leather coat kept him warm, but he still wore a pair of fingerless gloves.

People strolled down the street. Another without a jacket! They must be used to the harsher temperatures of this so-called heatwave. Low sixties was not the time to abandon jackets.

Some cruised and tried to make eye contact while others chatted with friends, paying him no mind as they meandered by.

The quarter buzzed with neon-lit nightclubs, throbbing music seeping out of their doors. Mixed in were quieter bars. Advertisements for friendly drag shows were posted in shop windows. Ni-chōme was the spot for queer people to gather, to be, and to be seen.

This wasn't home, but Sage could finally take his first deep breath since he landed in Narita Airport. He might not have been born here, and he didn't know any of the people passing, but here they were family, tied together by having a place on the rainbow. Each was connected by something deeper than birthplace, something encoded inside, linking them together, and it reinforced his belief he was doing the right thing with Kashi-sei.

So why was he playing with fire?

The answer stood across the street, waiting to cross. The light changed. Damn, Daiki had a sexy walk. He had changed into dark jeans, which clung to him, and a deep purple button-up shirt. His disheveled hair looked like… yup. Daiki dragged his fingers through the strands again, and Sage enjoyed how that made his hair appear tangled, like he'd just gotten laid.

Mm, attachment issues didn't seem that much of a downside. The need to guide Daiki's head to the side so he could trace his tongue across Daiki's neck and Adam's apple assaulted Sage. Gliding his mouth along Daiki's shoulder, he'd mark him so no one but the two of them would know.

If there were boxes of what attracted Sage, Daiki checked all of them and then some. It was the *then some* that caused the worry.

Today in the meetings, Daiki had excelled in asking the right questions and soothing Sage better than anyone ever. Ha, the fact that Daiki understood when he was upset…. Hell, most of his friends back home didn't pick up on it unless he became unhinged.

So sex between the two of them wouldn't only be knocking against a sexy body—their connection felt real. Not a good thing when Sage's intention was to avoid any such complications.

Daiki being so tightly held together, not emotionless but restrained, didn't help Sage's resolve not to go there either. Sage had a bit of a healthy fetish for turning someone's control off by tipping their world upside down, and the more controlled they were the better. He longed to see an untamed version of Daiki. What would that be like?

Damn, he couldn't blow off one of the most basic rules of business: you don't screw your coworkers. He shouldn't, couldn't, and wouldn't. Oh, but he so wanted to fuck Daiki, suck him, lick him, do all the things to him, with him, and for him.

Something told him Daiki didn't do casual, so Sage really *shouldn't* go there. If he needed to get his dick attended to, he should manage it without being stuck with a boyfriend.

Though imagining Daiki hurrying toward him on a regular basis wouldn't be a hardship. Not at all.

Keep it professional!

Daiki glanced at his phone quickly and then asked, "I didn't keep you waiting, did I?"

"Nope, right on time." He tried to stop smiling but couldn't. Daiki was even punctual.

"Where do you want to go?" Daiki looked around like he was the tourist.

"I'm not sure, but one of my friends said 7-Eleven needs to be our first stop so we can prime the pump." Sage wanted the full experience.

Daiki's nose scrunched in the cutest way. "Prime the pump?"

"That's what a friend of mine calls it. He recommended drinking a couple of cans of the 100 yen before hitting a club." The point wasn't about whether he could afford expensive bar drinks, but there was a certain principle and ritual he wanted to observe. And, well, the novelty of buying cocktails from a convenience store seemed like something he shouldn't miss.

The indulgent smile Daiki gave him made Sage want to see every kind of smile Daiki had, and he longed to have them all for himself. He stopped dead. How had he lost track of the beat? Maybe because he didn't know what song he was trying to play....

Daiki tapped his phone for a second, and a map showed where the 7-Eleven was. He pointed down the block. "This way."

The rainbow flags waved in front of bars, and music spilled out, welcoming them down side streets. Billboards on how to prevent HIV lit the way. Lockers lined the walls outside the dance clubs to store personal belongings, bags, and jackets.

People zigzagged between clubs. It was a decent crowd for a Thursday night.

The orange-and-green sign beckoned them.

Sage stepped through the door Daiki held open for him into the 7-Eleven. The windows and walls had a lot of posters, many of which were of bands being promoted. Others were various anime characters. Apart from the anime posters and some different varieties of products, the store looked pretty much like the ones at home—except for the extensive refrigerated section of alcohol. So many varieties of fun cocktails screamed out to him from their colorful cans. They got a couple each.

Once outside Daiki popped his open. "*Kanpai!*"

The toast meant dry cup. When in Japan.... "Bottoms up." His own poor choice of words made him snort because, as appealing as that was, no one's bottom would be up. He slowed his drinking until he could swallow without choking.

Daiki squinted at him.

He waved him off. "Immature, dumb joke. Kanpai!"

They pounded back their second can and then put them both in the recycle bin before they continued down the street, past several neon-lit stores and restaurants.

As they turned down Naka-Dori, the number of people grew. It was an average-looking street for Tokyo, but there were lots of standing signs on the sidewalk, directing people to their interests. These advertised massage parlors, restaurants, and various types of bars. Some of these bars included escort service, if Sage was understanding that correctly.

"I heard if someone hands you a tissue, they are really asking for you to join them in…." Sage's mouth failed him as Daiki's eyes widened.

"Asking you to join them in… what?" Daiki asked as he peered up the stairs that led to a bar.

Why did Sage even bring that up? "Um, sexual activities."

"Oh." Daiki nodded as if trying to find a place to store that information.

Each bar and club had their own cluster of people in front. Some groups were dressed to the nines, toasting with colorful drinks in fancy glasses, and in front of other establishments, people were laid-back, just sipping their beer.

Sage scrambled for something to say. "They are able to serve alcohol outdoors?"

"Of course."

As they walked past a bar, two blonds stumbled out, laughing and kissing.

Daiki's wide-eyed glances evolved into him stumbling to a stop to stare at the two men against the building. Public displays of affection weren't something Sage had ever seen much of in Japan. Though he couldn't imagine *not* bumping into people having full-on sex outside of some bars in LA.

He'd seen hand-holding here, but his parents had taught him public displays of affection were a tad tacky and simply not done. However, this fed his taboo-breaking nature, making the tiniest gestures of physical affection in public huge.

Sage never understood why visitors couldn't respect the cultural differences. Although isn't that what he was doing with the band? Damn! "Um, we can go someplace else if you'd rather."

"No." Daiki stiffened and pressed his lips together.

"You sure?" Sage might be reading him wrong, but he'd bet the tension in Daiki's body was caused by the allure and not censure of the forbidden make-out session.

"Yeah. I'm trying to be someone I'm not…."

"Who's that?"

Daiki whirled around to stare at him. "I said that out loud?"

The cuteness in this tall, handsome man would do Sage in for sure. "Yes. Who are you trying to be?"

"Someone who takes risks. And goes for what they want."

So Daiki was attempting to step out of his comfort zone. Sage found that intriguing and wanted to help… a little too much.

As they passed another bar, a guy tried to hand Daiki a beer. "Here you go."

"Sorry, I'm with a friend." Daiki pushed his hands into his pockets.

The man grinned. "I can be your friend, mate."

Annoyance wound through Sage. God, he hated pushy men. They shouldn't be throwing themselves at Daiki. Sage was standing right here.

"I can be your *best* friend," the guy persisted. Either he was drunk or stupid.

"He's with me." Sage threw an arm around Daiki to clarify the point.

After a visual groping, the guy purred at Sage, "Oh… I can be your friend too."

Daiki pressed his body to Sage's, fitting perfectly against him.

"I think not. Have a good night." Sage guided Daiki around Mr. Irritating. They passed two other bars and a club. He recognized the name as one of the places Ryder said should be on his must-do list. "Let's go in there."

Daiki nodded.

Sage put his jacket in a locker and then hiked up the stairs as the trance music got louder.

After the ID checks, Sage pointed to a prime table in the corner. The wooden seats had a view of the lightshow that flickered across the dance floor but appeared tucked away so conversation might be possible. The room was a combination of bright colors and mirrors.

"I'll get us… the specialty drink of the house?" After a nod from Daiki, Sage went to the well-stocked bar. The bartender was backed up, which gave Sage a chance to take a peek at Daiki.

Daiki seemed mesmerized by the various same-sex couples on the dance floor, and not exactly comfortable, if his squirming was any indication.

Had he misread Daiki? Maybe Daiki wasn't gay or bi or—

Sage needed to apologize. He got back to the table, and after Daiki thanked him for the colorful drink, Sage jumped in. "Hey, I'm sorry I assumed you're gay or at least bi."

Daiki showed him all his pretty teeth. "Are you asking? Because no one ever asked me that before."

"I'm sorry. I'm stumbling." This was worse than having no spares when he broke his drumstick during his solo in front of his entire high school. Fear threatened to choke him, but he buried that memory.

Daiki twirled the umbrella from his drink. "I am."

Stupid happiness abruptly replaced Sage's distress, like this was the best news ever. And why was he blushing? He could feel his cheeks catch on fire. "Ignore me. Give me a drink and I'm all kinds of ugly American."

"Or three." Daiki reminded him of the prime-the-pump drinks.

"Sorry I got nosy." Sage grinned.

"I don't mind." Daiki glanced down but smiled back up at him with so many of his needs and wants laid out like notes on a music score.

The hungry look lit something in Sage, so he asked, "How many partners have you had?"

"Well, other than a couple of girlfriends in high school and one in manga college at Kyoto Seika University, I haven't really dated."

"So no boyfriends?" Sage tried to keep disbelief out of his voice.

"Oh… um, no."

Maybe he was a one-off kind of a guy. "You stick mostly to hookups and—"

Daiki's gasp informed Sage that he was way off base with his free-loving assumptions. Partly this made him happy, but another part reminded him that was another reason to keep things business-friendly.

Frowning, Daiki shook his head. "I really haven't had much time for relationships, and being a mangaka doesn't really lend itself to meeting people."

"From what I understand, you're always on a tight deadline."

Nodding, Daiki said, "That's true, but you must think I'm lame."

"I think it's cool." He envied the man Daiki eventually played discovery with, but that would not, and could not, be him. That would be bad… on so many levels.

Daiki snorted. "Cool? That I have so little experience?"

Time to backpedal a bit and maybe get some distance from romancing the idea of being his first. "Actually, yes. Most guys I've dated have been around and are jaded."

Toying with the paper umbrella, Daiki frowned. "So you've dated a lot."

"Some. Nothing really serious." Sage didn't know why he hesitated with his information. He'd been with a fair number of guys, but nowhere near the average for a gay man in LA—at least according to Ryder.

"Really?" Daiki leaned back and stared at him.

"Yeah, why?"

"You're smart, funny, and a very great-looking…. Sorry." Daiki shook his head and refocused on spinning the tiny umbrella.

"Nice to be appreciated." Especially coming from someone as lovely on the eyes as Daiki.

"Come on, I'm sure lots of guys tell you you're…."

"What?"

"You know…." The shyness creeping into Daiki's voice did things it shouldn't to Sage.

"Actually, I'm run-of-the-mill. Nothing special in LA. I'm not famous, and I can't make anyone a star. Therefore I'm not of much value."

"I don't believe that." Daiki said it with such sincere conviction Sage wanted to help him with a taste of really stepping outside his comfort zone, if only once….

No! Bad idea.

Daiki pounded back his drink. His eyes had a dreamy quality to them, and his body was loose. Was he drunk?

He leaned into Sage, resting against him. "It's probably a super bad idea to tell you I find you attractive and very easy to be with."

"What?" Oh God. Everything in Sage started responding. He needed less talking. The DJ broke into the trance music and switched to a popular song. "Let's dance!"

Once on the dance floor, everyone seemed to want to get close to Daiki. He frowned and appeared to be a bit overwhelmed by the crush of people, or maybe it was Sage who wanted to keep people away.

Since he had *foreigner* emblazoned in his every move, Sage nudged two men out of the way to get to Daiki. He grabbed Daiki's hand and tugged him to a corner of the dance floor. Sage stopped himself from grinding on Daiki because this wasn't the place for that. But the way Daiki wore his desire in his eyes made Sage want to think about a place—

"I can tell you're a musician," Daiki called out.

"Why?"

"The music seeps into your body and seems to be forced out through your liquid movements. Thick liquid, like the way a good paint coats the canvas with one swipe of the brush, turning everything another shade."

Daiki wasn't only an artist with pictures but with words too.

"No one has ever said anything like that to me." Sage tried not to be ridiculously touched, but he was.

Pressing his lips together with a glint of determination in his eyes, Daiki said, "I can't imagine why not."

"You're going to make my face red," Sage tried to joke, but the way Daiki stared at him with such longing wasn't funny.

Sage swallowed hard around the affection bubbling out from his heart. He'd been with guys who said all the right things but never one who actually meant them. He reached out slowly, giving Daiki a chance to step back, but when he didn't, Sage wrapped an arm around Daiki's waist and tugged him closer.

Dance floors, wherever in the world, allowed you to be in public but alone in your world of two.

Daiki moved in perfect sync with Sage. They shifted, rocked, and glided, but their bodies were still teasing inches apart. Why couldn't he take his gaze off Daiki's?

Sage wanted him. It was that simple and that complex.

After forever, or maybe two more songs, the dance floor started to clear out. How late was it? Someone tapped Sage on the shoulder. "The last train is in twenty minutes."

Sage muttered, "Thank you," and gave a quick bow.

Daiki didn't look pleased, but then his face morphed into a grin. "You want to come over to my studio and see my manga collection?"

Sage opened and closed his mouth at Daiki's come-do-me expression. The shameless eighteenth-century come-on of using art as justification still worked its magic. Manga... etchings....

No, he couldn't. "Yes, I'd love to."

His dick was on board, as were his lips and mouth, but his brain screamed, "Bad idea." At the same time, his heart said, "What could it hurt?"

I shouldn't be going to his studio. I know that's his apartment. What am I doing?

"The train station is this way." Daiki had his phone out to guide them.

Sage pulled his coat out of the locker.

Fuck the trains. He waved and called out, "Taxi!"

"It'll be a hundred US dollars."

Sage shrugged. He'd have paid a thousand, because the sooner they got behind closed doors, the better. "It's on me. Just give him the address," he said as he pulled a shocked Daiki into the back seat.

Daiki did so and then sat back, pressing close to Sage even though there was plenty of room.

Chapter 7

AFTER SEVERAL attempts, Daiki finally pushed his apartment key into the lock. Over the course of the taxi ride, he'd sobered, but now nervousness threatened to get the best of him. He let Sage in.

"Nice place."

Sage stepped inside and moved over to the bookshelves filled with Daiki's stories. Stories he'd love to act out with Sage.

"It's small, but it works as a studio and living space."

"Bigger than my apartment was in LA." Sage glanced around the former living room turned manga studio at the monitors, keyboards, art equipment, and chairs scattered among the horseshoe-shaped desk area. "How many assistants do you have?"

"Currently four, but I'm interviewing for a fifth." Especially in light of recent developments, Daiki needed to get on that.

Sage pointed toward the wall of manga again. "Are these all yours?"

Pride at his accomplishments wound through Daiki. "Yeah."

"Wow. Floor-to-ceiling manga. May I have a look?"

Daiki flicked on the light near the bookcases.

Sage studied the shelves. He traced a finger over them as he muttered some of the titles out loud.

What the heck was Daiki doing inviting Sage back to his place? He really was taking channeling one of his characters a bit too far. Daiki's longing to be like some of his creations was more about his wanting to be that hidden part of himself. He wanted it to be seen and heard… by Sage.

It wasn't right that a man of twenty-seven was kissing his own hand to see what lips would feel like on skin. Practicing french kissing by moving his tongue around his own mouth so he'd have a better understanding of what his characters were feeling seemed wrong… especially when there was a gorgeous man standing in his studio who seemed ready, willing, and able.

Sage pulled out one of the volumes that was quite graphic. As he skimmed the pages, a slow grin transformed him into pure temptation. He turned toward Daiki. "This is incredibly hot."

He pointed to a place in the story where the character's bad decision would affect the rest of the manga. Everything had built to this point, and now the wrong move would—

Maybe Daiki had always been too careful and tentative. Akihiro's words echoed through him. "Some of the best stories are based on disasters." Daiki knew full well if he were to act on his feelings….

Think less and act more.

But how could he have the skill to not only fuck Sage up against a wall but have him begging for more? This wasn't a storyboard he had any experience drawing.

He shouldn't do this—he should think this out—he should…. But Sage was staring at him, clear-eyed and with an inviting lift of one eyebrow.

The part of Daiki's brain that manifested into his characters took over and promised he could live out his desire.

Daiki spun Sage around, protected his head with his hand, and then slammed him against the bookcase.

Sage's "*Oomph*" turned into a soft moan.

They were the same height, chest-to-chest so their bodies lined up—toe to toe, knee to knee, erection to erection, mouth to mouth.

Daiki could almost taste the sweet cocktails on Sage's breath. He stared into Sage's warm eyes, which issued a delicious dare wrapped in an invitation.

Sage hooked his fingers into Daiki's belt loops and tugged him closer.

Daiki arched for more and then wrapped a leg around Sage's thigh, which made his erection slide over Sage's bulge.

This was it. Did he back away, or did Daiki act on every instinct that told him he should go for it?

He cupped Sage's handsome face in his hands and found there a longing that had always been echoing through him as well. He traced a thumb over Sage's plump lips.

Sage licked over Daiki's thumb, erasing the lingering doubts of *shouldn't* and *bad idea*.

Daiki's mouth crashed onto Sage's. Lips parted and tongues collided in a wet, messy meeting. It was like nothing he had ever imagined.

Excitement threatened to overwhelm him as joy surged in him. He wrapped his arms around Sage for stability and ran his hands up Sage's back. Sage's muscles and contours were firm.

Sage pulled away and moaned as he unbuttoned Daiki's shirt. Sliding a gentle hand underneath the T-shirt, he continued to study Daiki until his gaze felt like a physical touch.

What did Daiki do now? He unwrapped his leg, but Sage held him snug against his arousal. Sage traced his hands over Daiki's body, his torso. His lips glided along Daiki's neck, sending spirals of need through Daiki.

Daiki pressed his lips together, but bits of aroused need escaped in gasps. Heat built between them. He needed to get Sage closer but didn't know what to do. "Please," he begged, not really sure what he pleaded for other than more.

Sage trailed his hands farther under Daiki's shirt and caressed the bare skin of his stomach, then skimmed down, tracing the waistband of Daiki's jeans.

It was like Daiki's carefully ordered colored pencils spilled out of their place all at once.

Sage didn't unbutton Daiki's jeans, but his fingers teased up along Daiki's ribs and circled Daiki's nipples.

Daiki hadn't realized how sensitive they were. He squeezed his eyes shut, focusing on the sensations of want and need roaring to the surface. Of course he'd drawn men having their nipples played with, but—

"Oh!" Rocking into Sage, Daiki cried out when Sage pinched each tip as Daiki thrust his erection against Sage's.

"Look at me," Sage demanded in a husky voice.

Complying was easy. Daiki simply opened his eyes, but now he was trapped in Sage's gaze once more. He swallowed past the impossible desire to stay right there, disconnected from everything and everyone except for Sage. Desiring to wrap himself around the man and not let go overpowered reason.

Reality slipped away to the edges where it no longer mattered, allowing him to do what he wanted.

Grabbing on to Sage tighter, he fused their mouths together as he walked backward toward his bedroom, pulling Sage along. His lips clung to Sage's even as he knocked into a chair and then bumped into the doorframe. Finally, he maneuvered them into his bedroom. When the back of his knees hit the bed, he spun them so the bed was behind Sage.

Sage drew his mouth away. "Should we—"

Daiki kissed his "Yes, we definitely should" into Sage's lips and with his trembling fingers managed to open Sage's jeans. The material was tight, so Daiki went to his knees to tug them down, taking the black jockstrap to Sage's ankles as well.

Looking up at Sage, Daiki took a mind picture. Sage stood there flushed, with his shirt on, naked from the waist down. His erection jutted out from a neatly trimmed dark patch of hair. A clean fresh scent along with something Daiki could only describe as male made him ache.

No censorship rules hid Sage's shaft, so Daiki appreciated everything. The length of him, the veins that lined his shaft, and the small teardrop that escaped from the head were not erased as they were censored out in BL drawings. He refocused and stared up at Sage.

"Can I?"

Sage blinked and then gave him a jerky nod.

Daiki wrapped a hand around Sage's cut shaft. He was hard, but much warmer than he'd expected. How many times had he erased the droplet seeping from the end of an aroused shaft? He couldn't resist, so he ran a finger over the tip.

Sage groaned.

He had caused that. Daiki repeated the motion.

"Mm." Sage shifted but let Daiki do as he pleased.

Daiki saw the circumcision scar and dragged his wet finger across the bundle of nerves, making Sage gasp and give him a smile.

"My last test of a few weeks ago came back with no issues. I'm on PrEP. So if you want to blow me, I'm not going to say no."

"PrEP?" Right, they needed to have a discussion.

"HIV preventive." Sage supplied reality.

He'd seen the billboards. Daiki took a deep breath and released the air over Sage's shaft.

Sage gave him a low-pitched groan that fed something deep inside Daiki. "Oh, you are a tease."

"Is that what I am?" Daiki asked seriously, but the look on Sage's face suggested his honest question fell on the erotic side without meaning to again.

Maybe being himself didn't prevent Daiki from starring in his own BL fantasy. Plenty of uke virgins sucked semes… or maybe uke sucking uke didn't matter as long as he got Sage in his mouth.

Daiki stroked Sage slowly.

Excitement warred with worry, which competed with affection and outright fear of rejection. He'd drawn these scenes thousands of times, but he'd never experienced the depth of emotion accompanying being on his knees for another man and wanting to be allowed to please him.

He longed for the connection taking Sage into his mouth promised. He had written more than one oral-sex scene ending in heartbreak plots—he might even be drawing himself into one right now, but that didn't stop him. Lust paled in comparison to the emotional and spiritual need to join with Sage… even if it was only temporary.

Daiki had never done this, but Sage was about to be the recipient of years of research. Time to put theories to a practical test.

"You don't have—fuck!"

Smiling, Daiki got a charge of power that soothed his ego when Sage reacted to his mouth. Following instinct, Daiki did exactly what he wanted. He licked Sage's hardness and bobbed his mouth up and down.

"Daiki, you look perfect with my cock in your mouth." Sage wrapped a hand around the part that wasn't in Daiki's mouth and stroked himself.

"Mm." Grateful for Sage's help, his words heating every part of Daiki, he still couldn't look at Sage. How embarrassing that he enjoyed having him in his mouth so much. He shifted on his knees, but that only served to tease him, not give him more room in his jeans.

Daiki redoubled his efforts. As he bobbed his mouth over Sage, his lips kept landing on Sage's stroking fist. He lost himself in a world of giving and want.

"I'm close… been a while." Sage's words sounded like they hurt coming out of his mouth.

Excitement tripped through Daiki. He sucked to the best of his ability, needing to make Sage come.

Stopping his fist, Sage asked, "Where?"

Daiki's mouth was full, so he pointed to his lips and kept sucking.

"Fuck yes!" Sage started stroking himself again, and with the other hand, he held the back of Daiki's head.

The sexiness of that move almost made Daiki come. He moaned around Sage's cock. Warm, salty liquid—cum—filled Daiki's mouth.

Moaning, Daiki swallowed. Some leaked out of the corners of his mouth and ran down his chin. He sucked steadily until Sage stopped coming. Then Daiki slowed and licked him clean.

He swiped a hand over his chin and licked his lips.

Sage groaned and collapsed on the bed.

What now? Daiki wondered. Should he—

Sage tugged on Daiki's hand. "Come here."

Daiki didn't resist. He crawled up the bed, but he couldn't quite meet Sage's gaze.

How should Daiki act? Finally he'd done exactly what he wanted, but now what? He tried to think of what one of his bolder characters would do, but his imagination abandoned him, leaving him vulnerable and shy. His cock ached, throbbing for relief, but embarrassment tackled him, and he was baffled as to what he should do.

Sage ran his fingers through Daiki's hair. "That was incredible. Can I?"

"What?" Daiki's voice squeaked, mortifying him.

In a quick move, Sage swung his leg over Daiki and kneeled above him, Sage's body straddling his. Sage sneaked a hand down and rubbed the bulge in Daiki's jeans.

"Ah," he moaned and thrust toward the attention.

"I don't want to embarrass you, but in terms of your history?" Sage's raked his fingers through Daiki's hair again, making him feel attended to.

He didn't know what to say.

Continuing, Sage said, "Are you on PrEP? If not, I want to use a condom even for oral."

A condom? Oh…. Somehow Daiki admitted, "I've never been with anyone."

Something flashed through Sage's eyes that Daiki would have identified as possessiveness and elation if he'd drawn one of his characters that way. "If you want to stop or want me to do something else, tell me."

Then Sage didn't do anything more. He waited. What was he waiting for?

Oh. Daiki gave him a nod of consent, but that didn't seem to be enough, so he added, "Yes. I will."

Sage shrugged out of his shirt, and when he leaned to toss it, he displayed breathtakingly beautiful angel wings decorating his back.

"Can I see?" He was harder than he'd ever been, but the artistic beauty of Sage's tattoo demanded satisfaction first.

Giving him a shy smile, Sage turned.

"Did it hurt?"

"Yeah, like fire spreading over my back." He looked over his shoulder at Daiki. "You can touch if you want."

Daiki caressed the warm skin of Sage's back. "The colors are so vivid. Red, orange, yellow, green, blue, and purple—it's the rainbow."

"Angel wings in Pride colors."

"They're gorgeous." Tattoos were rare in Japan due to the stigma connecting them to the yakuza, but he'd happily skip public *onsens*—hot springs—if he could just…. Daiki sat up and ran his tongue across one wing and then the other.

"Tasting the rainbow?" Sage laughed and turned around.

Getting the full meaning, Daiki muttered, "It's your visibility. Makes it clear this angel is on the rainbow."

"Mm." Sage was in a flurry of undressing activity.

Within a minute, Daiki's shirt and T-shirt were off, and his pants and underwear followed. Sage undressed him with so much confidence, it mortified and yet excited Daiki. But being with someone who knew what they were doing was a turn-on.

Daiki's erection, freed from its confines, waved proudly, and the wet tip had started to emerge from his foreskin.

Everything felt so…. He closed his eyes. He'd never been aroused and nude in front of anyone.

Sage pressed a soft kiss to his lips. "Remember to tell me if you don't like something or want to stop."

Daiki's "Okay" morphed into a groan as Sage wrapped his hand around him and stroked, sending shivers of lust through him.

"If you like that, let's see if you appreciate my mouth." Sage slid his body down Daiki, setting him on fire, until his mouth finally hovered over Daiki's erection, his warm breath caressing the head of Daiki's penis.

Daiki opened his eyes, but the vision of Sage licking Daiki's tip appeared through a starry filter.

Wet heat, along with the visual, cranked everything up to maximum.

Then Sage used his tongue to push back Daiki's foreskin.

"Oh." A whimper escaped Daiki, but he forced his eyes to stay open so he could witness the first time someone....

Sage cupped one hand around Daiki's scrotum and wrapped the other around Daiki's shaft. Staring into his eyes, Sage put his mouth over Daiki.

Hot. Wet.

Sage sucked him into his mouth and all the way down to his hand. So deep.

Daiki's eyes crossed as he breathed out, "Sage."

Suction.

Too much.

Too good.

No teasing. Sage gave Daiki everything he needed at the right speed. Fast.

Everything in Daiki had been coiled tight... forever. He tried to hold on to the elation, excitement, and pleasure, but the sensations were too much.

So close he barely breathed.

Sage sucked him in deeper and began to drag his lips up and down.

Shock waves hit Daiki. Pleasure rushed out from his core and echoed through him in satisfying surges.

Smiling around his full mouth, Sage bobbed his head as he swallowed everything he'd sucked out.

As the last bits of rapture tripped through Daiki, his entire body settled into a blissful contentment. He'd found paradise.

Once Sage finished licking him clean, he slid back up next to Daiki. He studied him for a moment and then pressed their mouths together. The sweet tenderness made Daiki ache for things only his characters ever got. The incredible ecstasy paled in comparison to the affection that now threatened to enlarge Daiki's heart permanently.

"How was that?" Sage wiped a thumb across his lips and grinned.

Daiki closed his eyes and hoped in the dim lighting Sage couldn't see how exposed Daiki felt. He whispered, "Very enjoyable."

Sage frowned for a moment and then nodded. "Was there anything I can do differently next time?"

"Next time?" Daiki squeaked. There would be a next time? He didn't think—

"I mean… you know, if we ever find ourselves…." Sage looked uncertain for the first time since they'd gotten into the bedroom as he backpedaled.

Daiki needed to cut out the crypticness. "That was better than anything I could have drawn. You have to forgive me. I simply don't know how to act… in this situation."

"Oh. Makes sense. Yeah, look, we can just be normal… yeah?" Sage sounded very Californian right then, even though he spoke in perfect Japanese.

Maybe Daiki wasn't the only one out of his depth. Afraid to ask, but needing to know, Daiki asked, "So what happens next?"

"Usually I leave."

Blunt and to the point. Daiki searched for a reason for Sage to want to stay. "Oh, um—"

"But I don't really want to unless you want to be alone and, I don't know, process or something." Sage gave him a little self-conscious shrug.

Daiki's heart filled with happiness. "No. Would you like some snacks?"

"Love some. I didn't have dinner. I wasn't sure… you know." Sage's confession made Daiki happy—he wasn't the only one too nervous to eat.

Sage flicked on the light next to the bed and stared across the gray room. Everything was shades of gray—bedding, curtains, walls—except for the picture across from the bed.

Oh no!

Getting out of bed, Sage pulled on his jeans. He stood in front of the picture Daiki had painted a decade ago. "Hey, this guy looks a bit like me before I bleached my hair."

Worry skittered through Daiki. What could he possibly say? Daiki went with the truth. "I've been drawing him since I was a teenager."

"What's his name?" Sage turned toward the bed.

Daiki took another mind picture, this one of Sage standing in Daiki's bedroom shirtless, with well-kissed lips and a relaxed, satisfied pose.

"He didn't have one…. Until recently." Daiki quickly pulled on some lounge pants and a T-shirt and said, "Let's go see what I have in the kitchen. One of my assistants usually makes sure the refrigerator is stocked up."

Sage grabbed him and gave him a deep kiss.

So much for avoiding what he was feeling.

Chapter 8

SAGE OPENED his eyes to soft light seeping in through the window. The all-gray room was silent.

Where was he? This wasn't his apartment, wasn't LA. Japan. He was in Japan. He was—he'd slept over at Daiki's? Holy—

Daiki was nowhere to be found, but a bottle of water and some aspirin sat next to Sage's cell phone, which was being charged. A now altogether too familiar feeling of sweetness coursed through him. Sage wasn't used to someone watching out for him. The sugary good feelings were ill-disguised affection, but before Sage could enjoy them, fear of getting used to such things chased the emotion away.

Last night after they had snacked, their conversation turned into sexy banter… at least on his part. Eventually Daiki, with the assistance of another beer, turned the conversation to sex. When the pros and cons of sixty-nining came up, Sage had the bright idea that experience was better than an explanation. Daiki immediately got on board, so to speak, and rode Sage's mouth to an orgasm while he sucked Sage off. Going all the way back to his apartment afterward seemed like too much trouble and a bit too lonely.

Oh shit!

He grabbed his phone off the nightstand and checked the time. Okay. Plenty of time to change before their first meeting.

Pulling on his clothing, he tried to think of something brilliant to say. He popped a breath mint, finger-combed his hair, then pulled an elastic out of his pocket to secure the hair out of his eyes.

He hesitated at the door. Argh! This was why he avoided the morning after with hookups. It was too weird.

The men were either arrogant, clingy, or simply didn't measure up in the light of day. What if Daiki developed virginal attachment issues? Sage's first experience with a guy had caused emotional confusion, so this was a possibility.

What had he done? Worry tackled him. What if now Daiki thought they were together? Why did Sage let his dick think for him?

He braced himself and then poked his head out of the bedroom. Hello, cuteness!

Daiki stared at a computer screen, wearing a fox hat and looking too adorable to be a mangaka god. As he glanced up, Daiki's expression brightened. "Oh, can I get you something to eat?"

Yes! No! Run! No. Should he be concerned that he wanted to stay… and not because he was hungry? But saying he would love to spend a little more time with Daiki wasn't right, so he said, "I was going to say I should get going, but, mmm, what's that delicious smell?"

"I reheated some pork with ginger. Let me get you some?" Daiki hurried to his kitchen area. He scooped some rice from the cooker into bowls and then added the incredibly aromatic pork.

"Sure." Sage ignored the foreign thrill of pouring tea for two.

Daiki smiled at him as they sat at his kitchen island. He pushed a bowl of rice topped with pork to Sage.

This didn't seem awkward at all. Daiki wasn't acting clingy or strange. He was simply Daiki. It had been Sage who was overthinking the situation. So what? They were two guys who got off a couple of times with each other.

It didn't have to mean anything, but… what if it did? A better question might be, could it mean something?

The adorableness of Daiki's headgear was—

Daiki followed Sage's gaze with his hands and touched his head. "Oh no!" He grabbed the hat off his head and set it aside.

The guys Sage had been out with before never blushed. He tried not to be charmed by how alluring Daiki's blush was as it made him the slightest bit pink from his cheeks to the tips of his ears.

"My fox hat helps me draw. Some of my assistants dress up as the characters they're working on or admire." Daiki's justifying scramble ended in a sigh.

"And not for nothing, but you look pretty cute in the hat." Smiling at Daiki, Sage tried to keep his feet on the ground. "Hey, I'm for anything that helps creativity."

He grabbed two pairs of chopsticks out of the cup on the counter and handed a set to Daiki.

Daiki ducked his head. "Thanks. My hat is from the Fushimi Inari Shrine, where my hometown is."

"That's the famous Shinto shrine near Kyoto, right?"

"Yes. The shrine is associated with foxes." Daiki gestured to his hat.

Sage tried to recall. "My mother's family is from Kyoto. I went there once with my parents. I don't remember much, but there are a lot of torii gates."

"Correct. They mark the transition from the mundane to the sacred."

They ate in a comfortable silence.

Why wasn't this weird? Any other time Sage would have had to do the walk of shame at a run, but there wasn't anything shameful about what they shared. He'd enjoyed exploring with Daiki. The man might not have had much experience, but he was a super-quick learner... an excellent student.

Sage liked Ikeda Daiki: the man who could really help him get Kashi-sei off the ground, the mangaka in charge of the manga meant to launch the band successfully, the guy who made him breakfast and wore a fox hat.

This is bad. Sage was in trouble.

Daiki peered at him. "Is everything okay?"

Had he sighed out loud? "Um, yeah. Sorry." Instead of obsessing over when this would turn uncomfortable, Sage had made it turn weird. He cleared his throat but not his mind, so he tried to change the channel his brain was stuck on with a question. "Do you really think Haru is right about Watanabe Wayuu and Suzuki Zen?"

Daiki was silent a moment and then nodded. "Being part of the band? Yes. They were both electric. They play multiple instruments. Their fans were fanatical, which wasn't a bad thing. Though they both seem hemmed in by idol expectations."

Sage chuckled. "It would be interesting to see their interactions working together."

"Mm, though I do worry about the tension between them." Daiki finished his tea.

"Though sometimes friction can be good." Why was Sage flirting?

Daiki peeked up through his lashes at Sage. "As you showed me last night."

Sage opened his mouth, but only breath came out.

Daiki's lips twitched, and then he pressed his pleased smile flat as he poured more tea for Sage.

Sage had to admit he liked this. Having breakfast with someone and just talking about things. He shouldn't get used to it. Perhaps he should count it as a win that last night's activities didn't appear to have damaged their relationship.

He put his dishes in the sink and cleared Daiki's. "I'm going to head out so I can be ready for our meetings."

Daiki walked him to the door.

Should Sage hug him? Bow? His parents certainly didn't say how to act on departing the morning after, and for all his research, no one had covered this topic.

"See you," Sage muttered as he escaped into the hallway.

Daiki followed him to the elevator, pushed the button, and waited with him.

Smiling, he gave Daiki a nod. Of course Daiki observed the custom of waiting until someone was out of sight before considering the goodbye over. Some of Sage's extended family practiced this as well. The gesture made him feel cared about.

Maybe he shouldn't enjoy having Daiki waiting for him to get on the elevator. Sage pushed the button again.

From the digital number appearing one floor up from them, the car seemed stuck there. The closest stairs were down the hall.

He glanced at Daiki.

Mistake. The sunlight from the hall window made his skin glow, reminding Sage of how smooth and nice he was to touch.

Finally the elevator doors binged open.

Now he didn't want to leave. He stepped inside.

Daiki grinned as if he could read the reluctance. "I will see you soon."

Sage nodded and waved.

Daiki kept waving until the doors were closed.

Oh wow! Sage put his hand to his heart and leaned against the back wall. How could such a simple thing mean so much to him? But it did. It totally did.

The mirrored walls of the elevator told him he shouldn't be concerned about Daiki's having attachment issues—maybe he should worry if he didn't.

Sage caught a cab back to his apartment. As Tokyo whooshed by, he couldn't help but feel whatever had begun to happen between him and Daiki was totally different from anything he'd experienced before.

Sage wasn't a player, but he'd been with a number of men. Most turned out to be pillow princes and were usually more work than fun. At least the men he'd met. They acted like he should be grateful for the privilege of being allowed to top and blow them. He didn't mind, but God, he wanted more.

Easy access had become boring.

Not that he wanted difficult or dramatic… or even a relationship, but meeting someone real with something other than becoming a star on their minds was nothing short of a miracle. The fact Daiki cared about making the world a better place—well, that was amazing.

Daiki was amazing… and Sage wanted more Daiki.

BACK IN another cab, Sage held his imaginary drumsticks and beat a happy tune in the air on the way to the meeting.

He stepped into the conference room and joined the three people already there.

Haru gave him a nod.

The agent stood and greeted him.

Sage could barely take his gaze off Daiki to return the greetings. Daiki wore a dark suit and a white button-up shirt with a purple tie, but what captured Sage's attention was Daiki's smile. His smile reached his eyes and was filled with affection. Warmth sparked fires inside Sage. "Beautiful… day."

The agent squinted and glanced out the window. "It's pouring outside."

The door opened, and Suzuki Zen stepped in.

Greetings, cards, and bows were exchanged. Everyone took a seat.

Across the table from Sage sat someone who would rather cut than speak politely, take than ask, and had the biggest chip on his shoulder Sage had ever seen, and since he'd grown up in LA, that was saying something.

Suzuki Zen was nothing Sage had expected. The demure singer always appeared mild and meek on stage, even when he had wild purple hair. He was soft-spoken… and gentle.

The Zen across from them clicked his thumb ring against the row of his ear piercings and stared at them with a dead expression. Then he finger-combed his dark shag-cut hair and glared at them. "Not what you hoped for, huh?"

Sage glanced at Daiki. He turned back to Zen and winked in exaggerated LA fashion. "I didn't say that."

"You didn't have to. I know the expectations people have, and I'm just no longer willing to pretend I live up to the innocent bubblegum idol that was created."

"Good…." Sage wasn't sure how to word it. "I'm looking for artists to be themselves. I don't want a group of stereotypes meant to pander to an audience or societal expectations. I want—"

"Yeah, until the label presses you or the bottom line doesn't meet your target goal."

Sage opened his mouth, but Daiki touched his hand and chimed in, "That's why he is doing Kashi-sei without assistance from labels or sponsors."

"I've heard you're pouring your own money into this. Really?" Zen eyed him.

"Yes."

Zen studied him. "Why?"

"Whether it's here, America, Europe, or the Middle East, music has the ability to get past the bullshit society tries to dish out. Music is always on the forefront of change."

A little of Zen's defiance seemed to drop with his shoulders.

Sage didn't have the luxury of not being totally honest. "And it broke my damned heart to lose Fire and WTZ."

Zen straightened, and his face scrunched up. "*Pff*, Fire. They were nothing."

Daiki's mouth dropped open as he stared at Zen.

Haru chuckled.

"What? Compared to WTZ? Ha! Fire was nothing but flashing lights and fancy dance moves."

"You can't cut Watanabe Wayuu's talent." Haru pointed out the obvious.

"And I never would. His voice is a rare and precious gift. He has the ability to embody song." The reverence in his voice was duplicated in his expression and then disappeared like notes in the air. "However, the rest of the Fire members lacked talent. Fire were decent to look at, but they didn't have anything other than gymnastic dance moves... and Watanabe Wayuu."

He wasn't completely wrong. None of the other members had seemed truly interested in music; they'd been more interested in capturing more fans by appealing to mass expectations.

Zen used his chin to indicate he spoke directly to Haru. "I've heard you just have to play the music once and it's yours."

Haru rolled his eyes. "You heard wrong."

Dropping back in his seat, Zen shook his head. "Nah, a bunch of bands say that."

The smirk Haru gave him was a mix of fuck off and I'm fucking with you. "I only have to *hear* the song and it's mine."

"Nice... and modest." Zen nodded, appearing impressed and then trying to cover it.

"Who says you can't be more than one thing?" Haru grinned at him and then directed his focus back onto Sage.

Daiki also stared in Sage's direction.

Sage went into his well-worn spiel about Kashi-sei, but Zen leaned forward, not bothering to hide his interest, and that made Sage hopeful. He ended with, "I want Kashi-sei to be more than just an idol band. I want our music to make a real difference. I'm not in this to make money, though if it puts anyone's mind at rest, one of my dad's financial analysts says we would probably break even in the third year."

"And this is worth it to you?" Zen stared at him.

Daiki interjected, "Suzuki-san, have you heard his YouTube channel?"

"Call me Zen, and actually I have. But Sage, how do we know you won't get bored and fold in a month?"

Sage returned the favor of pointing out the obvious. "After you signed with WTZ, how did you know that band wasn't going to break up in a month?"

Zen shrugged. He frowned at the detail page and then spun the paper in a circle.

"The salary is to compensate for loss of future potential income." Sage needed to be up-front.

Exhaling hard, Zen stopped the twirling page. "It's generous, but the scope of this...."

"It's intense," Daiki added. "And a risk. Everyone involved is taking a chance."

Good, Daiki! How did he say so little but make the maximum impact?

Zen studied each of them in turn. "Are you asking me to join?"

Nodding, Sage clarified, "I wouldn't have wasted your time if we weren't sure you'd add to Kashi-sei."

"But why would you consider it?" Haru asked the most important question.

Zen hesitated. He grabbed the water bottle in front of him and drank slowly. Recapping it, he pushed the bottle back to its original spot.

Sage bit back a smile. The singer's ability to hold an audience's attention even while sipping water was impressive.

Tilting his head at the agency representative, Zen asked, "Can this stay in this room, just between Kashi-sei members?"

Sage gave her a nod.

"I'll return shortly." Maybe she realized she wasn't adding much value, or perhaps she wanted deniability later on.

"I should—" Daiki stood.

Sage grabbed his hand. "You may not play an instrument, but you are part of Kashi-sei."

After a moment of what looked like indecision, Daiki sank back into his seat.

The door clicked closed, and Zen said, "My sister is X-gender and is dating a girl."

Wanting to make sure he understood, Sage asked, "That's similar to the term nonbinary?"

Haru nodded. "Yeah, basically. X-gender is not adhering to the gender binary. Zen, what pronouns does your sister use?"

"She hasn't done anything other than to tell me. I want my sister to be able to live as she wants when she's ready. So I'd be doing this for her." Zen looked down. "Plus... I miss it."

"The crowds and adoration?" Haru asked.

"Playing music... but yeah, the fans were great too. I miss working on new songs and singing. I miss being in a band." Zen's harsh mellowed even further.

Might as well know now, so Sage asked, "If we were looking to have two singers, any issue?"

Zen narrowed his eyes. "Depends on who."

Sage couldn't resist. "Who do you want to work with?"

Zen gave him a smirk and shook his head. "He'd never agree to it."

"Who?" Sage pressed him, because Zen coughing up an admission would go a long way in bridging the gap between the two singers.

"It's crazy after everything that happened, but I've always wanted to work directly with... Watanabe Wayuu." Maybe Daiki was making Sage use a love-is-in-the air filter, but he swore everything about Zen softened when he breathed out Wayuu's name.

"Aren't you pissed that what he said basically ended WTZ?" Haru studied him.

"He was only telling the truth. I am hot." Zen stated the fact with such a straight face Sage dared not chuckle.

Zen cracked up, and Haru joined in.

Sage asked, "Do you have time to meet with him?"

Zen sat up straighter. "Who? Watanabe? Is coming here? When?"

Nodding, Sage said, "After lunch, if you have—"

"I'll be here."

Daiki grinned at him, making Sage's heart full and happy. Things were clicking into place... on many levels.

Chapter 9

ON THE short walk to the restaurant, Daiki admired how easily Sage engaged both Haru and Zen in conversation. Several times, Sage caught Daiki's gaze and gave him a sinful smile.

Images of Daiki's wanton behavior last night splashed over the storyboards in his mind, leaving him aroused and more than a little impressed with himself. He had done what he wanted with whom he desired, and the world hadn't fallen apart.

Talk about living a BL fantasy. Daiki couldn't have drawn a better night. There didn't seem to be much morning-after strangeness between them. Even better was that Sage had implied they might be doing it again.

Shoving his hands into his pockets, Daiki readjusted himself. How could simply looking at Sage get him aroused like one of his needy ukes?

In the light of day, Sage had only a passing resemblance to Daiki's 2-D fascination. Sage was much sexier, and his personality twisted Daiki in circles. He was smart, easy to be with, kind, and while he respected traditions, his uniqueness satisfied Daiki's love for the unpredictable. His confidence was heady, and the way Sage used his mouth….

Sage licked his lips as if he could see the explicit pictures Daiki's brain painted in his head, both dirty and sweet.

After adjusting himself discreetly one more time, he held the door of the restaurant for the others to enter. Zen and Haru did so while Sage stood close behind him.

"After you." Sage's deep voice did unreal things to Daiki, and the way his breath tickled the back of his neck…. Mm, chills.

Daiki forced himself into the restaurant and didn't lean back against Sage to rub all over him.

Inside he sat next to Suzuki Zen, who had been one of Japan's top idols. Without his disguise of baseball cap and face mask, no one could say Zen wasn't handsome, but Daiki couldn't stop staring at Sage. Everything about Sage captured his imagination.

His mental storyboards kept flashing through his mind, growing more graphic and sweetly serious by the moment. He probably shouldn't crawl over the table to end up straddling Sage's lap, and—

"What may I get for you?" The waiter's tone suggested this might possibly be the third time he'd asked.

"Um, the chicken yakitori meal and the Kiraka White tea."

After they ordered, Daiki excused himself from the table. Maybe splashing some cold water on his face would calm him down.

Sage grinned at him, turning his heart inside out.

The bathroom was occupied, so Daiki stood in the hallway leading to the men's room and studied the abstract paintings. The artist had been angry when these were made. Didn't the restaurant owner feel that? Or were they simply trying to match red-washed walls?

A quick movement in one of the private rooms, adjacent to the hall where Daiki stood, caught his attention. An older man in a business suit grabbed another man trying to leave a booth and yanked him back.

Harsh words cut across the space. "If you think I won't release that video clip of you tied up getting your kinky ass beat, you've got another think coming. You owe me."

Did Daiki need his glasses? That couldn't be.... The guy being pulled around looked a lot like him, but he was dressed in a glittery pink T-shirt, not black leather.

The man ducked his head submissively. "I know. I just—"

"You'd better get into this band, Wayuu. I'm getting my money one way or another." The guy's growl worried Daiki.

Confirmation—that was their two o'clock interview being terrorized.

Watanabe Wayuu nodded. "I've got to go get changed."

"Go.... And be ready to pay me some of interest you owe me this evening." The words made Daiki's insides prickle with wrongness.

Wayuu sagged and sank back onto the bench seat. He shook his head. "You know I don't have any money."

"I'm not looking for yen." The suit's voice dropped into a lower range as if he were trying to convey sexy, but he came across all creepy.

"But—"

"I'm in the mood for the same as last time." The guy's sinister smile made Daiki's skin crawl.

Watanabe Wayuu pushed himself out of the booth and toward Daiki's hallway. Bumping into Daiki, he muttered, "Sorry," as he exited out the back door.

Daiki ducked his head and hoped the guy didn't get a good enough look to recognize him when they met.

BACK IN the conference room, Zen popped out of his chair and began pacing. He glanced at his cell phone. "When is he supposed to be here?"

"Two o'clock," Sage said as he fussed with the elastic keeping his hair back.

Daiki followed Zen's circuit around the room with his gaze.

Haru chuckled.

"What are you laughing at?" Zen growled.

Arching an eyebrow, Haru said, "You. Are you worried he's not going to show up or that he is?"

The door opened, putting Zen behind it.

Watanabe Wayuu stalked in and swiped off his sunglasses. His dark hair was feathered back from his face. He might have put a bit of eyeliner or mascara on, making his eyes the focal point. Even though this was a business meeting, he wore his leather pants and matching jacket over a tight black T-shirt like a rock idol fresh off the stage, making Daiki's fingers itch with the urge to draw him.

If Daiki hadn't seen a different side of him in the restaurant, he would have thought this was the true Watanabe Wayuu. The duality of subdued, submissive, and bullied versus rock legend was nothing short of miraculous.

The man who'd yanked him around the restaurant like a rag doll entered the room and introduced him. "Watanabe Wayuu needs no introduction, but I am Fumio Ito."

Greetings and cards were exchanged, but before they were finished, the agency representative whispered something in the man's ear.

She turned and said, "I'm sorry for the abruptness, but I must speak to Ito-san immediately."

"Of course, take your time," Sage said, as if it wasn't unusual to disrupt a meeting like this.

The two gave a quick bow and left the room.

When the door closed, Zen said, "I have a bet for you, Watanabe-san."

Heat seemed to slide across Watanabe's entire being, and the brightness could have eclipsed the sun if it hadn't been swapped in a flash for placid indifference. Watanabe's duality might short-circuit Daiki's artist's brain.

Watanabe did a slow turn to Zen and scanned him with his gaze. "Wayuu, please. That goes for everyone. And now, what would that bet be, Suzuki-san?"

Zen strutted forward and got into Wayuu's space. "Call me Zen. I bet you won't work with me."

Either way, it was a win for Zen. Win the bet or get Wayuu to join the band. Daiki needed to find ways in the story to highlight how well Zen used this strategy and was glad he was on Kashi-sei's side.

"I'll take that bet." Wayuu's words came out breathy. He cleared his throat and added, "That is, if the other members are interested in me… joining."

Haru smirked and leaned toward Sage and Daiki. "We should have some popcorn about now."

As inappropriate as that comment was—*Hello drama!*—Daiki had no doubt parts of this manga would be dictated; he would simply draw what he witnessed. At times, his manga muse was kind to him.

Zen folded his arms over his chest. "What are the stakes?"

Neither spoke—they only engaged in some sort of staring contest. The silence went on for a bit too long.

Finally Sage tapped the table. "How about the winner gets the forfeit of choice from the loser."

Wayuu glanced at Sage and stood straighter. Then his gaze traveled to Haru and to Daiki.

His eyes went huge as recognition wound through him.

Nothing Daiki could do would change that he'd overheard that mess in the restaurant, so he smiled, trying to reassure Wayuu, but Wayuu's face fell, and all his confidence seemed to deflate.

Wayuu hurried to sit in the empty seat.

Zen gave Wayuu an arched eyebrow. His expression was a mix of amusement and possessiveness. "It's a bet. I already know what I want."

Wayuu dropped his gaze and stared at the table in front of him. He chewed on his lower lip. Gone was the brash and bold personality who strutted across the stage, and only a quiet man who seemed lost and out of his depth remained.

Daiki found himself wanting to help. His mental storyboard simply opened a new window on the page, and a character redirected the conversation. He'd be that character. "Sage, why don't you tell Wayuu about Kashi-sei."

Sage jerked a bit in his chair as he dragged his attention from the intensity and snapped around to smile at Daiki. "Thanks," he said, and then he launched into his pitch.

Daiki had heard Sage's ideas of the band several times, but each time he got in deeper. He wished he could play an instrument. Picking up the pen in front of him, he smiled, glad he had a part to play.

Haru spoke up. "So, you interested?"

Zen leaned forward, obviously hanging on Wayuu's openmouthed pause.

Smiling as if it didn't matter, Sage said, "No pressure if you want to think about it."

"Are you serious about allowing each of us to be ourselves?" Wayuu's voice cracked.

Sage nodded.

Wayuu gestured to his clothing. "What if 'myself' is not leather and all dominance? Still interested?"

Zen smirked. "I especially want you to be you… because *I* am all dominant."

If Daiki had to capture Wayuu in that moment, he'd have drawn a puddle, but he'd never replicate that breathy little whimper Wayuu made.

Haru rolled his eyes. "Keep your domination to yourself, Zen. We gonna do this or what?"

Wayuu opened his mouth, but the door opened at the same time, admitting that man again, along with the representative.

"Before he accepts, let me see the contracts." Ito-san bumped into Wayuu as he grabbed the detail page off the table.

Sage frowned. "Are you his agent, Ito-san?"

Wayuu pressed his lips together, his eyes went big, and he shook his head.

The man shot daggers at Wayuu and then through clenched teeth said, "Manager, actually."

Zen studied Wayuu for a moment, then glared at the man. "Is that right?"

Ito-san turned over the sheet and cocked his head in Sage's direction. "I don't see a page for rules, consequences, or physical expectations."

Wayuu sank lower in his chair.

Shaking his head, Sage said, "There isn't one. We are all professionals. I don't—"

Ito-san's chuckle had a mean tone as he rested a hand on Wayuu's shoulder. "That's a shame. Wayuu does much better when there are penalties. Don't you?"

Grimacing, Wayuu shrugged off Ito-san's hand, shrank down in his chair, and stared at the table as if lyrics he'd need to memorize were etched into the top.

Sage frowned. "That will not be a part of this band, ever."

Shaking his head, Ito-san exhaled. Then he glanced around the table. "Suzuki Zen will be part of this band as well?"

Sage gave him a small smile. "If we're lucky. Yes, Kashi-sei will have two of the finest singers in Japan... if they agree."

"The world, actually, but I'm too modest to correct you," Zen deadpanned.

Wayuu turned to him with a cocked head and a grin that reached his eyes for the very first time since Daiki laid eyes on him.

"Yes, well... this seems to be reasonable." Ito-san looked up from the detail sheet.

Wayuu shifted away from the guy's hand when it tried to land on his shoulder again.

Ito-san said through clenched teeth, "We will meet tonight at seven to finish our *discussion*."

Daiki couldn't stand it. The guy and whatever hold he had over Wayuu felt incredibly wrong. "I'm sorry, that won't be possible."

All eyes turned to him... including Sage's.

It was a risk, and he wasn't even channeling a character, but he couldn't stop himself. As crazy as it sounded, he wanted to protect Watanabe Wayuu. "Sage wanted everyone to leave here and go directly to my studio for the night."

"For the night?" Haru and Ito-san asked at the same time.

Sage's warm expression had morphed into a wide-eyed stare.

Daiki sent *follow my lead* through his brain waves and eyeballs, along with a small nod.

"Yes, um, yes. It's incredibly important for us to begin to meld as a band as soon as possible." Sage pulled that out of nowhere, but it sounded credible.

"Yes, from this point forward it's Kashi-sei twenty-four seven for a few weeks, if not longer."

"Yeah, right." When Ito-san saw the firm set of Sage's chin, the expression devoid of amusement on Haru, and Zen throwing him death wishes with his eyes, he added, "Well, with this salary, I guess we're on your timetable."

"We're? Don't you mean Wayuu is?" Haru clarified.

Sage stood. "Thank you for your time today."

The company rep stepped in and led a bemused Ito out of the room.

Daiki smiled at the band. They had rallied around Wayuu, even if they didn't know why.

WHEN THEY slid into the car Sage had requested to pick them up, Wayuu sat beside Daiki.

"Give the driver your addresses so we can stop for your stuff." Sage smiled at Daiki but didn't ask any of the questions about the impromptu slumber party that were in his eyes.

Somehow Daiki had gained Sage's trust, and that made him feel great. They were playing on the same team, even though Sage wasn't clear on all the details yet.

Once the addresses were given, Haru asked, "For one night or…?"

Sage tilted his head to Daiki; his eyes were just—no, not the time to get lost in Sage's kind eyes. "Um, oh, I guess a couple of nights, right? The band will probably find an apartment quickly?"

"The agent has several apartments to show us. I'll see if she can do tours tomorrow. Sound good?" Sage glanced around.

"Great," Zen mumbled, and he stared out the window. "Hey, where will Kashi-sei debut?"

"Good question. I only know what was recommended to me. I obviously don't know the scene here."

"I'd be happy to help arrange some shows," Zen volunteered.

Haru nodded. "Hey, if it's not stepping on toes, I'd love to participate."

Sage caught his breath, but then he nodded with a smile. "Um, yeah, sure. That would be a big help. Thanks."

Haru and Zen had specific ideas, so a friendly debate began. Sage questioned them about locations and club owners.

When they got to Wayuu's apartment, he leaned in and asked, "Can you help me?"

Unexpected, but Daiki said, "Sure."

"I'll help you," Zen and Sage offered.

"That's okay. I'm closest." Daiki slid out of the seat and shut the car door before anyone tried to follow.

The apartment building was old and didn't have an elevator. Apparently Wayuu was used to this, as he bounded up the stairs.

Daiki hiked up the stairs a little more sedately and found Wayuu reading a notice tacked to his door.

"Is that an eviction notice?" That meant he was months behind in rent.

Wayuu shrugged and opened the door to his apartment. "Makes moving a good thing."

The small room was dark, so Daiki flicked the light switch, but nothing happened.

"Power was shut off a while ago."

Looking around the mostly empty room, Daiki tried to understand how an idol like Watanabe Wayuu lived here, but he failed. The tiny room had a kitchenette. A tattered sofa with bedsheets and a pillow on it, a lamp sitting on top of a cardboard box, a small scarred chest of drawers, a guitar case, and a shoe rack that had seen better days were the only furniture.

Wayuu glanced away from Daiki. "I sold everything to try to pay down Fire's debt. At least there's not much to pack."

He grabbed a suitcase plastered with tour stickers out of the only closet and began packing his clothing into it. "By the way, I know you overheard in the restaurant."

Daiki couldn't lie, so he nodded.

Wayuu shook his head. "I can't imagine what you think of me."

"That you're one of the most talented singers in Japan—ah, no, the world." Daiki smiled but failed to lighten the mood.

Wayuu gave him a small chuckle and went into the bathroom. He came out and added the few toiletries in a plastic bag to his suitcase.

"Fire's overseas tour was canceled, and because of that, the band got into debt. Ito-san rescued us. The other guys escaped, but I'm on the hook... and recently, Ito decided the money I owe him isn't enough."

"From what I overheard, he's using a private clip to blackmail you."

Wayuu crossed to the chest of drawers. He grabbed the contents out of the top drawer and added the items to his suitcase. "Mm, sounds like a plot in one of your manga."

For lack of anything else to say, Daiki let his "I'm sorry" echo around the empty apartment.

Shrugging, Wayuu opened the bottom drawer and smiled as he pulled out a framed picture. He traced his fingers over it and then turned to display the picture of Fire. "This was after our first big show."

Didn't have to tell that to Daiki. The band appeared to have made it, and they were floating in a sea of what seemed like unstoppable happiness. "We'll have to take one of your first big show with Kashi-sei."

"Mm." Wayuu set the apartment keys on the table, grabbed the suitcase that seemed to contain his entire life, and picked up his guitar. "Thank you," he said as he walked out of the empty room.

Once they were back outside, the driver took the suitcase and guitar. Daiki and Wayuu got into the car.

Sage reached over and buckled the safety belt around Daiki. His arm brushed across Daiki's chest. He paused right in front of Daiki's face.

Their mouths were so close.

Daiki's vision tunneled. Sage's lips were right there, and then Sage licked his lower lip. Daiki leaned toward heaven—

Tap, tap, tap.

Daiki jumped. "Oh."

Zen squeezed his shoulder in apology and then said, "Speaking of manga, tell us what you have planned for us, Sensei."

Manga? Oh, right. He was a mangaka, not the drummer's personal kisser, though if that were a job, he'd apply. Daiki smiled at how rare it was for someone to make him lose place and reason with embarrassing ease.

He turned to Zen. "Nothing too out there. The manga will focus on Kashi-sei's brand of visibility. I'll keep the storylines as close to reality as possible. I've already hooked into a couple of LGBTQ advocacy groups because I want to slide in information where I can."

Haru air-guitared a bit of a soundless song and then said, "Smart. They will also be a good source of marketing."

Sage frowned but then nodded. "I guess getting their input makes a lot of sense, considering what our mission is."

Daiki tried to keep calm, but when Sage got all—

"Will my little sister be able to read Kashi-sei's manga?" Zen asked.

Um… car with other people; not the time to get turned-on. Focus on the question. "Depends on her age."

"Seventeen."

"Definitely."

After quick stops at Sage's and Haru's, they pulled up to Suzuki Zen's luxury apartment building. A teenager appeared with an overnight bag in one hand and a keyboard in the other.

Zen jumped out of the car. Words were exchanged that Daiki couldn't hear. Zen kept shaking his head no, but the teen stamped her foot and wouldn't release the bag.

He dropped his head, grabbed his keyboard, and then stomped back to the car.

"Um, I hate to impose, but could you say hello to my sister, Sensei?" Zen handed Sage his keyboard.

"What? Oh, um, sure." Daiki stepped out of the car.

Zen whispered, "Don't mention Wayuu is with us. Otherwise— just don't."

Haru snorted, but Sage and Wayuu didn't add anything.

"Okay." Daiki smiled at Zen's sister as he walked over to meet her.

"Sensei, this is my sister, Suzuki Yumi," Zen introduced them.

They exchanged greetings. She gave him her card with all her details as well as her social media accounts.

"Please call me Yumi, Sensei. I love your work so much. You are why I want to be a mangaka." Daiki listened to her gush embarrassingly rave reviews for his work. Her compliments were flattering, but her brother was a rock star, and there was another idol in the car who had a big following—not to mention Haru, as well as Sage—so her praise felt as overwhelming as it was misplaced.

Daiki responded to numerous questions and even agreed to look at her work. "You can pass your drawings to me through your brother… if you don't mind, Zen."

Zen glanced at his sister. He chuckled. "I don't, but even if I did I don't think that would matter…. Okay, sis, we've got to go."

She tossed the duffel bag to her brother and waved them off.

"Thank you. You were very kind to her." Zen rested his head on the back of the seat.

Daiki still felt like his face was red. "I'm grateful to all my fans, but I was taken aback by her extensive knowledge of my work."

Sage smiled at him and squeezed his thigh for a moment.

Haru asked, "So why didn't you tell her Wayuu was in the car, or does she hate anything Fire, like you?"

Zen glared at Haru and then glanced at Wayuu. "For one, it would've been a thing—a very big thing—and secondarily, I don't hate all things Fire at all…. Not even a little bit."

Daiki wanted to say something, but a bump pressed him against Sage, and he allowed himself to enjoy the closeness.

Chapter 10

SAGE HELPED clear the dishes Daiki's assistants brought in for the band as Daiki broke out the sake.

The way in which Daiki served, using two hands to pour from a brown-and-blue earthen *tokkuri* carafe, did odd things to Sage. The ritual of sharing sake was a small thing, but Sage treasured someone who appreciated the intimacy and performed the traditional activity so mindfully.

When Daiki stood in front of him, Sage held his *ochoko*—the matching cup—on his fingers, supporting it with his other hand.

As soon as everyone had been served, Daiki returned the tokkuri to rest on ice in a chilled larger vessel with slow, practiced movements. The ritual relaxed and enchanted Sage. He nabbed the tokkuri, then carefully filled Daiki's cup. He added sake to the vessel, put it in the ice, and took the seat next to Daiki.

Weird how he relaxed simply feeling Daiki's body next to his. It was—

Haru elbowed and side-eyed him. "You look happily confused."

Sage shook himself and held his cup out. "Thank you all for making this dream one step closer to reality. Kanpai!"

As everyone shouted, "Kanpai!" he caught Daiki's gaze and mouthed, "Thank you."

Daiki's eyes fluttered shut for a moment, and then he gave Sage a shy smile and mouthed back, "Thank you."

Happiness filled him and freed him the way only drumming had in the past. He drank and held the cup, waiting for Daiki to refill it. Once Daiki replenished everyone else's, Sage poured Daiki's and topped up the tokkuri.

The talk became easier once they were on their second bottle of sake.

"Tell us about dating in LA?" Zen leaned toward Sage as if he wanted all the salacious details.

What could he say? Glancing at Daiki, who also seemed to be interested, made Sage shrug. He didn't want to talk about before, but he said, "Dating always felt like auditioning."

Wayuu snorted. "Playing a part. Always pretending to be what you're not."

Everyone stared at him.

Sage had been referring to the number of would-be actors in LA, but....

Swallowing the remaining sake, Wayuu waved them off. "What? Everyone pretends to be someone else."

Nodding to help Wayuu move past that bit of unexpected truth, Sage added, "Like emotionally stable."

Chuckling, Haru shook his head. "Hey! Some of us are emotionally stable. Ask my girlfriend."

Zen slid his gaze over to Wayuu. "I find someone who has it all together rather boring."

Haru looked between the two of them and inclined his head. "To each his or her own." Sagging a bit on the counter, he asked, "Question, Wayuu. Who exactly is Ito-san? I know he's your, what… manager? But—"

"He owns my ass." Wayuu snorted.

Zen set down his cup harder than usual.

Wayuu picked up the tokkuri, handed Zen the cup, and refilled Zen's ochoko with a shaky pour.

Zen wiped his sake-wet hand on his pants. "He picked up Fire's debt?"

Sage hadn't heard much on the subject but bristled at the thought of being at that man's beck and call.

"Looks and brains," Wayuu murmured as he folded his arms on the counter. His head fell onto them two beats later.

Zen swiped some strands of hair out of Wayuu's closed eyes. "Wayuu. Watanabe Wayuu?"

Haru chortled. "He's down for the count. Anyone heard of Ito?"

Pulling his attention off the passed-out man, Zen snatched his lingering hand away from Wayuu's hair.

Daiki shifted in his seat and stared down at his sake.

Sage studied Daiki and tried to read between his actions to what he wasn't saying.

Zen frowned. "Ito is one of those various investors who cares nothing about the music, only the money and power controlling a successful band or idol can bring."

"You've just described the music business globally." Sage didn't bother to keep the annoyance out of his tone.

Sitting straighter, Haru asked, "But he wouldn't—"

"Why not? It's not a secret how some idols are mistreated behind the scenes," Zen answered, pointing out the horrid reality Sage didn't want to be a part of. Trying to improve that situation was why he was here.

"You?"

"WTZ's agency wasn't terrible, but I had my share of issues and run-ins." Zen shook his head as if to shake off the memories, and pounded back his sake.

Haru dragged his fingers through his hair as he grimaced. "I guess Freddie Mercury's assertion wasn't wrong. And you and Wayuu probably know this more than most."

Zen squinted at him. "What?"

"Freddie said that maybe we're all musical prostitutes. Giving the fans what they want, when they want it, for money…."

Sage shook his head. "No musician should have to pay with their soul."

"Or body." Daiki covered his mouth as if he needed to stop more words from falling out.

Zen's hands on the counter tightened into fists.

Refilling everyone's cup except Wayuu's, Sage held his up. "Never. Kanpai!"

Everyone conscious said, "Kanpai."

"What should we do about him?" Haru pointed to Wayuu.

"I've got him." Zen gently shook Wayuu, and when he didn't wake, Zen pulled Wayuu's arm around his shoulder. Wayuu roused out of unconsciousness enough for Zen to half carry him to the second bedroom.

Sage attempted to help, but a glare from Zen made him back off, so he took on the supervisory role of pulling down blankets, adjusting pillows, and trying not to laugh at Haru's snarky comments.

Haru's eyes sparkled with mischief, but he kept a straight face. "Don't give me that look. I simply asked if you'd be tucking us in as well?"

Zen growled.

Biting back a laugh, Sage exited the room and returned to the kitchen.

Daiki had cleared the counters and was straightening everything.

Sage rested his chin on Daiki's shoulder and leaned in for a moment. "You knew?"

Daiki didn't look in his direction but gave him a nod. "I overheard something I shouldn't have at the restaurant."

"That's why you suggested this sleepover and why Wayuu asked for your help getting his things?" He really wanted to know what Daiki and Wayuu had talked about but tried to sound like it didn't matter.

"Yes." Daiki started the dishwasher.

"Thank you for breaking out the sake." Sage tapped a beat with his hands on the counter.

Daiki shrugged. "I find it helps my assistants tell me what they really think."

Sage stopped drumming and stepped in front of Daiki. Their gazes locked, and Sage fell into an oasis filled with everything he'd ever wanted.

He cupped Daiki's face and lifted his chin, putting Daiki's lips in line with his. Their breath mingled, tantalizing him. Anticipation of touching those lips again—

A door opened, and Daiki stepped back. He turned and busied himself with rearranging the dish towel.

Haru came in rubbing his eyes. "Oh, sorry. Just coming in for some water."

Daiki got four bottles out of the refrigerator. He handed one to Haru, and Sage accepted the other three. "For Wayuu and Zen. Have a good night."

Sage didn't want to go, but Haru stood there like he was watching a play. Sage asked Daiki, "Um, do you think you could come with us tomorrow on the apartment search?"

Daiki's eyes got huge like one of the characters he drew. So damned cute!

"You'll be staying with us a lot of the time… right?" Sage's dad would have been impressed with how he loaded that question. Maybe he should have been shocked by his desire to do so, but being close to Daiki chased away anything except the need for more.

"Um...." Daiki looked around the apartment as if it held a usable answer.

Haru's body shook with a suppressed chuckle.

Sage shot Haru a look of "Help a buddy out and stop being a cock blocker."

Giving Sage a slight nod, Haru said, "How else would you be drawing us realistically?"

Daiki opened his mouth, but Sage wasn't sure what the answer would be, so he quickly added, "We'll leave around eleven. Night."

He escaped into the bedroom before Daiki could say no and found Zen staring down at the sleeping Wayuu.

Sage clearing his throat seemed to propel Zen to the other bottom bunk. "You and Haru get top bunks."

"Sure." Sage wasn't sure what was going on between the two singers, but his real issue was that a top bunk would make sneaking out more difficult.

DIFFICULT BUT not impossible.... Sage grinned as he made his way through the dark living space over to Daiki's room. The bedroom door was open a crack, and the light was on.

Daiki sat cross-legged on top of his comforter in lounge pants and no shirt. His hair was every which way under his fox hat, and the round-framed glasses made him look hot like a delicious schoolteacher, smart like—

"Oh, Sage." Daiki ripped off his hat and glasses.

What was it about Daiki that turned Sage inside out? Sweetness, intensity, talent, a willingness to explore—

Daiki tilted his head. "Did you need something?"

Sage closed and locked the door. He traced a finger over Daiki's lips, which were far from innocent now, and answered, "You."

"Me?" The surprise in Daiki's voice tripped another wire in Sage's brain, tightening the cords around his heart.

Sage licked his thumb and glided the wetness over Daiki's bottom lip. "You look like you're ready for me."

Daiki's eyelashes fluttered, and he whimpered the tiniest bit. "I am."

Wow. "I like that you don't play games."

Daiki licked Sage's thumb. "When my characters aren't honest, all that does is create drama."

"You don't want drama?" Too many men did.

"No."

Sage really believed him. "You want something other than drama?"

"You… I want you. Right now. Please." His honest need and sincerity couldn't be ignored.

Sage shouldn't let himself fall so fast, but glancing at Daiki, who wasn't hiding the affection, he clipped the usual strings that held him in place. Besides, Daiki was impossible to resist, and Sage didn't want to.

He tangled his fingers into Daiki's hair and smelled the strawberry scent of his shampoo. Sage kissed the hair he held. He wanted to kiss everything.

Daiki twined his arms around Sage and pulled him down on top of him.

It would be so easy to just take this where they wanted it. Daiki's total surrender was there in every shaky breath he took.

No, not the time. Sage dragged his mouth along Daiki's neck and kissed his Adam's apple.

Daiki's gasp wasn't loud, but Sage didn't know how thick the walls were. He whispered, "Shh," in Daiki's ear, which seemed to have the opposite effect.

Sage tried to get off him, but Daiki's hand skimmed down Sage's back and settled on his ass. He thrust up as he pressed Sage's ass down. The thin material of his lounge pants and Sage's jersey shorts did not prevent alluring friction from making too many promises.

Daiki stared up at Sage like he was everything, and it was too much.

He captured Daiki's mouth with his own and kissed him. What started out as soft and slow turned into hot and fast.

Their rutting had all the finesse of a high school make-out session, but the feelings were new and real and had Sage getting desperate. He needed to take this up a notch or they'd both come hands-free.

Reaching into Daiki's pants, he wrapped his hand around Daiki's erection and gave him a stroke.

"Yes. Sage. Yeah." Daiki got the words out between the kisses and slipped a hand down the front of Sage's shorts. His tentative touches became gropes, which finally evolved into nice firm tugs.

Dear Lord, when had Sage gotten so hot over a hand job… but this was Daiki. Daiki's breathy murmurings and purrs had him right on the edge.

"Quiet. We've got to be quiet," Sage whispered as he swallowed down his own groan of excitement. The impossibility of keeping this a secret teased his kink for the forbidden, and he craved more.

Daiki nodded, but his moans suggested he didn't understand the meaning of Sage's words.

Sage was on the cusp. Daiki's shaft leaked and throbbed in his hands, proving he wasn't alone in this insanity.

"You want to come?" Sage asked, as if either of them had much choice. Crossing the finish line was a foregone conclusion.

"Yes," Daiki pleaded, and he sped up his fist.

His panting turned into a long moan as he came.

Sage covered Daiki's mouth and tried to swallow his whimpers of completion. But when his own orgasm pulsed out of him and into Daiki's fist, he lost all hope of controlling anything, least of all his groans. He rode the wave of pleasure until it finally ebbed.

SAGE WOKE to the most delicious sensation… a sleeping Daiki in his arms. Daiki snuggled in and then rolled over and clutched a pillow. Sage watched him breathe, and he let a sense of peace surround him like a weighted blanket.

He could get used to this, and he wanted to wake up holding Daiki every morning.

What a weird want. But wonderful nonetheless.

Sage used the bathroom and then wandered over to stare at the painting. The image bore a passing resemblance to him, and in this dim light of dawn, he did see many similarities between himself and the picture. Should his ego be stroked that he looked like Daiki's dream man or worried that Daiki might be just living out a decades-old fantasy with him?

Way to be paranoid.

Sage headed into the kitchen.

Daiki would be hungry when he woke up. Sage couldn't make much, but he could make fried eggs. Afraid of the grease splattering on his bare chest, he put on the apron that hung on a hook. He reheated some leftover vegetables, made some eggs, and poured tea.

With everything balanced on a tray, he slipped back into the bedroom.

Daiki sat in bed and set aside his sketch pad. His hair was almost neat, so he must have freshened up. "Oh, Sage. Don't move."

"What? Why?" Sage didn't know what to make of Daiki's demand as he pushed the door shut.

"Can I take a picture of you?" Daiki pleaded, as if snapping a photo of him was of dire importance.

"What? Why?" That knocked him sideways. He needed some new questions.

Daiki grabbed his phone and took some shots. "You, shirtless in the apron, carrying a tray... I can't draw you fast enough because I want to enjoy you immediately."

"Are you okay?" Sage had never made anyone breakfast before, especially not in bed. But if a breathy artist totally hot for him was the usual reception, he'd have to make Daiki every meal.

Shrugging, Daiki nodded. "Yeah, I'm not used to being in a manga that I'm drawing."

"What?"

Daiki groaned and touched his face. "I'm going to have to tint my cheeks with embarrassment lines."

Ah, got it. Sage played along. He made a show of looking where the blanket failed to hide Daiki's arousal. "Oh, by the way, you're drawing not only yourself but me very aroused."

Daiki put down his phone and pushed off the comforter. He didn't meet Sage's gaze, but the shifting of his body highlighted his jutting erection, not disguised at all by the shorts he wore.

"A gorgeous man bringing me breakfast in bed...." Daiki frowned and shrugged it off, then pasted on a teasing smile. "You probably make breakfast in bed for your lovers all the time."

Sage's desire to actually get someone who wanted him for him seemed to pull out the truth. He should stop himself from the long stare, but couldn't. Instead he confessed, "No. I've only done this for you."

A million expressions crossed Daiki's face, but a predatory one stayed. "This is a first... for you too?"

Swallowing, Sage clutched the tray tighter. "Yeah."

Daiki slipped out of bed and onto his knees in front of Sage. "May I?"

What was he—

Daiki ducked under the tray, pushed the apron out of the way, and grabbed on to the waistband of Sage's lounge pants. He peeked out and tilted his head, making hair fall into his eyes. "Sage?"

His name never held so many questions, but there was only one answer. "Yes."

Smiling a real smile, Daiki shifted forward and disappeared, hidden by the tray Sage held.

A hot, wet mouth wrapped around him and sucked him halfway in.

Sage hardened fully and gripped the tray tighter. "I should set this down."

Daiki appeared not to have heard him, because he continued sucking him. Adding his hand, Daiki started stroking Sage in an enticing rhythm.

Something out of the corner of his eye made Sage turn his head. There was a full-length mirror behind the door, giving him a view he'd never had. How had he become the star of a filthy manga? But Daiki looked too beautiful to be associated with anything dirty. Sexy, yes.

The reflected image seared into Sage's brain. Him getting a blowjob while clutching a tray, and Daiki sucking him, with a hand busy down the front of his pants, while he stared at Sage.

Their gazes caught in the mirror, the uncertainty in Daiki's eyes dragging Sage deeper into his thrall. Daiki wasn't conducting some elaborate game of seduction; it was clear he simply wanted to suck Sage and get off.

No question Daiki had stepped way out of his comfort zone and was exploring what he wanted... and right now that was Sage. That might have knocked him sideways, but it was what Sage wanted too.

Sage's affection for Daiki was a nonstop fast beat. His feelings hadn't evolved slowly over time in a measured fashion but had appeared in a moment. Had he been waiting all of his life for someone to open his heart? Maybe he'd get burned, but he couldn't stop being consumed by the driving rhythm because surrender felt too good.

He gripped the tray tighter. The predicament of having to hold the tray while getting sucked off increased his arousal. So far, only a little bit of the tea had spilled on the napkins. Could he come without dropping the tray?

Turning back to the mirror, he stared as Daiki bobbed his head, bringing the wet heat of his mouth up and down with ever-increasing suction. Sage had never watched himself getting sucked off. The act felt new and forbidden; not being able to see Daiki except in the mirror added to the uniqueness.

He hadn't locked the door, and three other guys were a room away. The worry of being caught in the act intensified everything.

Sage wasn't going to last long, so he warned, "Close."

Daiki pulled off him, gave him a shy smile, and started licking his shaft. Long, wet, well-placed licks were going to—

"Oh God." As he came, the tray wobbled in his hands, but he held on and let the pleasure pulse through him.

The fact that Daiki came too, moaning as he shot off, made Sage's experience perfect.

When he could move, Sage set the tray on the nightstand and pulled Daiki off the floor.

"You're incredible." He kissed Daiki because how could he not?

Daiki pulled back. "I must taste of—"

"You do." Sage tugged him back into a kiss and pushed his tongue into Daiki's mouth.

He guided Daiki over to the bed and broke the kiss. "I think your breakfast might be cold."

Daiki gave him a sheepish grin and then licked his lips. "My breakfast was delicious."

"Oh…." Sage didn't know what to say, so he focused on getting the tray to the man he was falling in love with.

He sat next to Daiki and pointed at the picture. "I'm grateful to bear a passing resemblance to your ideal man."

After kissing Sage's cheek, Daiki leaned in to him and whispered, "There's nothing passing about you or this."

ZEN HAD chased everyone out of the shared bedroom so Wayuu could sleep. Though Sage doubted anything but a marching band would wake the guy up. When he'd gone into the room to grab his phone, Wayuu was sleeping hard.

He smiled at the shirt he'd borrowed from Daiki's closet. Sharing clothes was a symptom of relationships… and he was good with that.

Across the main room, Daiki bent over his computer with his glasses and fox hat on.

Sage couldn't help but hope to borrow Daiki's clothing for a long time.

Daiki's assistants had started coming in around nine.

Sage met each one and embedded their names into his head. They were an important part of Daiki's world, and therefore his.

He stood near Haru and Zen, who were skimming the titles along the bookcases.

"Did you read manga growing up?" Sage studied the cover of the manga he held and got the appeal.

Haru nodded. "I grew up reading another artist."

Zen wandered over. "My sister reads manga too. She says sometimes the presentation can be problematic, but it saved her life."

Haru nodded. "Mine too."

"How?" Sage asked, wanting to understand.

Pulling out one of the books, Haru said, "It expanded my world view. And even though I wasn't exactly like the characters, seeing people who were different made me feel less lonely. Even the imperfection of it gave me space to be. They gave me hope to keep going."

Zen smacked Sage on the back. "That's what Kashi-sei is going to do, right?"

"I sure the hell hope so." Sage grinned and glanced over at Daiki, who was staring at him.

As soon as Daiki recognized he'd been caught, he ducked closer to his computer. Too cute.

Chapter 11

DAIKI TRIED to focus on his assistant, Takahashi Ichiro. This newbie wanted to burn down the entire system with one match, and Daiki tried to follow his rant, but then Sage laughed at something Haru said.

Sage has such a nice laugh. Not forced but deep, and the sound made squiggles of happiness spiral through Daiki.

Akihiro nudged his foot against Daiki's. *What? Oh.* "I'm sorry, could you repeat that, Ichiro?"

The newbie hesitated and then nodded with a big grin. "You're right. I need to rethink everything. Thank you, Sensei. Thank you."

Daiki pressed his lips together and pointedly ignored Akihiro's openmouthed stare. If his words helped encourage someone else to answer their own question, there was no problem… right?

A short time later, the real estate broker took the band and Daiki on a tour of the luxury apartment, which was within walking distance of Ni-chōme.

The window seat called to him, so he opted to stay in the apartment as she took the others around the building to show them the amenities, which included a full gym, sauna, and pool.

Daiki curled up on the built-in white cushion. A gorgeous view, and the light was perfect for sketching. He flipped open his pad, picked up his pencil, and let the graphite fill the page. His grandfather had labeled his pads and pencils Daiki's his protection against the world. Maybe so, but seeing life through the lens of his drawing allowed everything to be more palatable.

The sharp angles of Sage's face forced his hand. He'd done drawings of poses Sage seemed to favor—leaning back in his chair, what he looked like asleep, and how angelic he appeared when he came.

He couldn't focus on that here, so he changed to a sketch of the band.

"What are you drawing?"

Daiki jumped at Haru's question. He turned the pad around to show him. "You."

"Kashi-sei. Wow, look at us," Haru gushed at the quick sketch of the entire band on stage.

Daiki smiled. "It's not finished," he said as he turned back to the page. He needed to add a touch of shadow along—

Someone cleared their throat.

Sage asked, "So would you help us decorate?"

Daiki glanced up and found the entire band and real estate broker staring at him.

How long have they been standing there?

He set his sketchbook aside. "What? I mean, of course. But decorate what?"

The real estate agent pointed across the room. "I have catalogs on the counter. All you have to do is pick furniture, colors, and the accents. After I call the order in, everything can be delivered within five hours."

"We can move in tonight?" Wayuu asked with so much hope it hurt Daiki's heart.

Zen stepped closer to Wayuu. "Of course we'll be living in each other's pockets from now on."

Blushing, Wayuu stepped away from Zen and stared out the glass doors that led to the balcony.

Sage chimed in, "Yes, I don't see why not. If everyone likes this place—"

"Wonderful. We only have paperwork and furniture choices to make." The broker smiled, probably at her commission.

Daiki couldn't stop meeting Sage's grin with a small smile of his own. He liked the idea of being in Sage's pockets… in his pants… in his bed. *What is with me?*

Sage's lips quirked like he could read Daiki's dirty thoughts. He pointed to the real estate agent, who shuffled paperwork. "I'll go sign the leasing agreement."

Watching him moving across the room was—

"Since we already set aside the one room for practicing, do you guys mind if I take the single?" Haru asked.

Zen nodded. "Of course you should have the single. You've got a girlfriend. Wayuu and I can share the larger room on this side of the apartment, and Sage can have the one at the corner."

Wayuu gave Zen a big-eyed stare but didn't say anything.

Flashing Daiki his idol smile, Zen added, "Good light in the bedroom on that side of the apartment for you. Besides, I'm sure you and Sage won't mind sharing."

"No, of course not." Daiki mumbled, trying not to be embarrassed that the other guys might have heard him and Sage this morning *sharing* his bedroom. "Um, so we should look at the decorating books."

Sage glanced up from reading the rental agreement. "You guys pick what you want. It's covered, but keep in mind the living room will need to double as a dance studio."

The real estate agent was on the balcony making some calls.

"Haru, what's your style?" Daiki couldn't begin to guess.

Haru scratched his head. "I don't know. It's been whatever me and my girl could afford. I guess I want something warm, soft, and inviting, like my girlfriend."

Zen grimaced. "You mean cozy. Geez, you weren't kidding before when you said you were straight."

A growl and an angry glare came from Wayuu. "Stereotype much?"

Snorting, Haru said, "He's not wrong, though. I don't know whether to be insulted or complimented."

Shaking his head, Zen said, "Neither. Just put me down as observant."

Daiki wanted to get confirmation. "How about soft textures in creams mixed with gold. Chests of drawers and a shallow desk in honey-colored woods."

Looking at the pictures Daiki pointed to, Haru nodded. "Yeah, I like that."

"I think these two chairs will fit in that nook between the window and the en suite bathroom." Daiki thought it would be a nice place for the two of them to relax when they wanted to get away.

"Yeah, that sounds great." Haru's tone said he was trying to summon excitement for Daiki's sake.

Zen pointed at Sage. "Now, Wayuu, I bet you LA Drummer-san will have exact opinions on his decor."

Daiki bit back a smile. "Isn't that another stereotype?"

Zen shrugged. "It's another bet."

Wayuu asked, "But are you stereotyping people from LA, gay men, Americans, or—"

Rolling his eyes, Zen patted Wayuu on the shoulder. "Allow me to finish. I'm stereotyping Sage. Let's just say I'll bet he's going to let Daiki make the decision."

"We'll see. What's the bet?"

Smirking, Zen answered, "To be determined by the winner."

"These bets are adding up." Haru grinned; he appeared to be keeping track. "I'm going to call my girl. Any issue if she spends the night?"

Zen waved him off. "Have at her."

Haru snorted. "Don't let her hear you say that."

Daiki began the task of pulling information from Wayuu and Zen.

Wayuu shook his head. "Whatever you think."

Daiki couldn't tell if he was speaking to Daiki or Zen.

Zen held the color wheel up to Wayuu's face. "Which goes best, Daiki?"

"Goes best... with Wayuu?" What an odd question.

"What color bedding would he look best against?" Zen turned on his idol smirk and winked.

Wayuu gasped, then played it off. "Stop teasing, Zen."

"Never." Zen stared at him until Daiki cleared his throat. Turning with a raised eyebrow to Daiki, he asked, "What about white on white on white. Very minimalistic."

That was easy enough. Daiki asked, "Wayuu?"

Wayuu tore his gaze off Zen and smiled at Daiki. "Sure. Sounds good. Easy to keep clean."

Zen guided Wayuu toward their new bedroom. "You plan on getting things dirty? Well, let's see where the bed goes."

"You mean beds... don't you?" Wayuu's voice cracked.

"Whatever." Zen smirked, then added, "but if we had one bed, there would be enough room to also have a small table and two chairs, right?"

Daiki wanted to be careful. "Um... yes, but maybe Wayuu—"

"No, I'm good with sharing. I actually have a hard time sleeping without someone in bed with me." Wayuu's voice got softer with every word he said.

Zen's mouth dropped open, and then he folded his arms over his chest.

"What? I got used to having someone sleeping next to me when I was training to be an idol and then in Fire. We always shared a bed. Didn't WTZ?" Wayuu scowled at Zen.

Softening his expression with an almost shy smile, Zen put a gentle hand on Way's shoulder. "No, our band didn't, but I have no issue sharing with you."

Wayuu gave him a tiny nod and then meandered back to his assigned room.

Zen stumbled into a chair trying to follow. He straightened the chair, gave Daiki a gesture that indicated he was going, and then trailed after Way.

That settled that… at least as much as things between those two were going to be.

Daiki shoved aside the plot bunny those two birthed and made some notes. He gave the information to the Realtor and promised to send the rest by email as soon as possible. She said her goodbyes.

Sage grabbed the keys from the Realtor and walked her to the door.

He hurried back to Daiki with a big smile and handed him a key. "For you."

Holding the key in his hand seemed too big. "I don't need—"

"Why not? You'll be living here… at least part of the time." Sage's gaze got intense, making all the tubes of paint in Daiki's mind gush.

Safe topic needed. Daiki asked, "Um, what color would you like your room?"

"*Our* room. I heard Zen giving Haru the other single—"

"Do you mind, because I'm sure—"

"I've got no issue, and I'm glad I didn't need to arrange it… unless you've got a problem sharing with me."

Daiki shook his head emphatically. "Not at all. I…." No games! His face grew warm, and his cheeks probably tinted with crimson, but he finished his thought. "I'll enjoy sharing with you."

Sage leaned in. His lips were so close.

I could drop to my knees and—Daiki jumped back. "Um, so what colors do you like?"

"You choose for us." Sage put the emphasis on *us*.

Daiki had to admit he liked the sound of *us*. He'd never really been part of an *us*. Did this mean they were dating? Or sleeping together? Maybe both. Were they boyfriends? If not, how did that happen? Did Sage want that to happen?

Perhaps his storyboard should have less desperation drawn into these frames.

Maybe, but this was better than the smell of his first manga straight off the press. He'd be living with Sage. They could do what they'd done this morning and more… anytime they wanted. A shiver of excitement painted him with exhilaration and anticipation.

He needed to stop staring at the rainbow wheel of possibilities for answers.

His grandfather had been right; Daiki turned to art when things got too real.

How to decorate a room for Sage? Daiki had always migrated toward soothing shades since he didn't want to interfere with his art. Had he been living behind a filter that only let certain tints in? Was he ready for…? He needed to stop hiding.

After meeting Sage, he'd found having brilliant, vibrant colors didn't diminish his art but enhanced his creativity and gave it new direction.

Although not caring about color and its impact on a space, well, that was a crime. Choosing one said a lot about a person. "Wait, Sage. Um, you don't have an opinion?"

"No, I trust you. You know what I like."

A distant "I win" from Zen echoed in the empty apartment.

Trust. *Sage trusts me.* Maybe it was a small thing, but having the trust of someone he'd only met—last week, though it seemed like so much longer—was an incredible gift.

Pushing aside all the emotions that started swirling, Daiki cleared the noise and saw tubes of paint. Maybe one shade wasn't enough for Sage. He had brought a rainbow into Daiki's world. "How about a kaleidoscope of color?"

"I like that."

Pleased, Daiki nodded. He could do the rainbow, like Sage's wings. "Your room should be a haven as well as a reminder of your mission."

"Our room," Sage added with a grin.

Daiki sputtered but then remembered one of Sage's videos. "Wait, do rainbows annoy you?"

Sage pushed some of Daiki's hair out of his eyes. "No, only when advocacy stops there."

"Oh, okay. So, a multitude of colors…." Daiki flipped through the comforters and decided he'd match the furniture accordingly.

Picking one that looked like a rainbow rained on the bedding, Sage asked, "Do you think a king bed would fit?"

"I... I...." Images of what they could do on a bed that big flooded his thoughts. Many of his sexual fantasies threatened to tackle him.

"I bet it will. What do you think for the living room?" Sage changed the subject, possibly out of mercy, which Daiki appreciated since fainting from lack of oxygen to the brain would be bad.

Good. Safe subject. "Since the apartment is an open design—the kitchen is all white with stainless—that color scheme could be echoed in here. A mirror against this wall with a huge flat-screen behind one of the corner sections, along with any electronics or gaming consoles."

"Nice, like a secret panel." Sage chuckled.

Daiki could see it all. "White sofas and chairs in a durable leather that can be easily moved against the wall. I saw the book had silver and mother-of-pearl cabinets, and accent tables with shallow profiles. I'll order the general kitchen package, which would include all-white china, glasses, utensils, pots, and cooking things. As well as bathroom sets and towels for each of the guys matching their bedrooms."

"Sounds great." Sage pointed to the wall where the sofa would be. "And for here, maybe you could make a picture of the band?"

"Yes, I'd love to."

"EVERYTHING LOOKS great. Take a break and sit with me so I won't be lonely." Sage pulled Daiki to one of the apartment's new love seats and sat with him, keeping close against his side.

"We are all here, Sage," Haru snarked.

"Right, but he's the only one that matters to Sage." Zen held his hand palm out. "No need to deny it to save our broken idol hearts."

Daiki grinned and shook his head. Sparks of relief flicked through him. Was that the band's way of telling him they accepted his relationship with Sage...?

Zen kicked back on the love seat next to Wayuu. "Well, that was an impressive day."

Wayuu shifted away, putting space between them.

Sage gave a single clap. "Okay, let's discuss the practice schedule."

"What time do people wake up?" Haru asked.

"I'm up early, but I'm good working my schedule around everyone else. As long as I get some time with my sister, I'm good." Zen edged a bit closer to Wayuu.

Wayuu didn't move away, kept his gaze focused on Daiki, but smiled just a little.

Haru shrugged and said, "I usually sleep late after a show, but otherwise I can set an alarm. Ichika is usually up early."

"How early are we talking?" Sage traced his finger along the embroidered tiger design on Daiki's jeans, reminding him of how Sage preferred they start their day.

"Let's say ten… thirty?" Zen stared at Wayuu as if he were trying to read his mind.

Wayuu nodded. "Sounds good to me."

Sage said, "Great. Every day except Saturday we'll practice. Anything else we want to discuss?"

"Since everyone is here," Daiki said, deciding now was a good time, "I wanted to touch base with you on the manga."

All heads turned toward him.

How was this his life now? He pushed away the fact that two of these guys were idols and the other two were on their way to becoming ones. And best of all, he and Sage…. "Um, as I get into drawing more of the storyboards, I'll ask for your input. I want you to be comfortable with how you're represented on the page."

Haru cocked his head. "Hey, aren't you the artist? Most artists don't want anyone impacting their creativity."

Daiki wanted to gently correct this opinion, which was held by most people. "While artists may be free to draw anything, it doesn't mean we should. Creativity and the freedom to use it doesn't mean there aren't consequences."

Sage tilted his head and stared at him. "The contract gives you basically total discretion."

Daiki had made sure of that, but he glanced around the group. "But this band is made up of real people who live in the world beyond my manga. I want to be careful how I'm representing each of you. Visibility—being seen—is an incredible concept, but some things are private and aren't meant to be shared."

"Makes sense," Zen said.

"Thank you. I—" Wayuu jumped when his phone buzzed.

Even from where Daiki sat, he could see the upset on Wayuu's face as he stared at the screen.

"Who is it?" Zen asked.

Wayuu shook his head and sent the call to voicemail. As soon as a beep alerted him there was a message, the cell phone rang again. He directed that call to his messages as well. Another alert sounded, and then his phone rang a third time.

Zen stared at him and then asked, "Don't you think you should get that?" in a gentle voice.

Wayuu shook his head. When the phone rang one more time, his hands were shaking so hard he dropped the device.

Zen fished between the cushions to retrieve the cell. He glanced at the screen and grimaced. "It's Ito. Don't you want to—"

Wayuu shook his head hard. "No, I know what he wants."

"What?" Sage leaned forward.

In a very small voice, Wayuu said, "Me."

"What!" Zen glared at the phone.

Haru set his drink down. "You want to tell us?"

Daiki hoped the emphasis on *us* reminded Wayuu he wasn't alone. The band were going to sink or swim together, so they all needed to understand what was happening.

Wayuu took his phone from Zen and played the message on speaker.

"Wayuu! You owe me. Where are you? Answer my calls or I will post this clip within twenty-four hours. You want your fans to know Watanabe Wayuu is a kinky sub who sluts it up at parties?"

Closing his eyes, Wayuu said, "He sent me the clip… of me… at a BDSM party…."

"That bastard," Haru growled.

Wayuu sighed and shook his head. "The clip has me on a St. Andrew's cross. I should just quit the band. I don't want—"

"Absolutely not," both Sage and Zen said at the same time.

Haru followed with "No way."

Zen gave Sage a nod, then a small smile.

Daiki wished there was something he could do. He muttered, "You need to own the narrative."

"How?" Wayuu's voice broke.

Sage started pacing. "Yes! What if we…? No, but maybe we could—"

"What?" Zen demanded.

Following Sage's train of thought easily, Daiki nodded. "That might work."

"What?" Zen asked again.

"What if we do a BDSM photo shoot? Echoing the clip?" Sage's idea gave them something to rally behind.

Zen snapped his fingers and pointed at Sage. "Wait, didn't a K-pop group do something like that a while back? They even had a Master-sub contract in with the DVD set."

"We don't even have a song." Wayuu's voice was barely above a whisper.

"Might not be necessary, though it'd be nice," Sage said.

"I can do a sneak release of Kashi-sei in one of my ongoing BL series. Introduce Kashi-sei while you're at a BDSM party. A couple of frames of a couple of you, including Wayuu, in various submissive poses. The premise could be the party evolves into a shoot, or vice versa."

"I love it." Sage kissed him on the head. "I can do a vlog about the nightlife in Tokyo and add a few pictures teasing the song."

"What about the song?" Haru asked.

"Do we need one?" Zen tilted his head and smirked. "Or do you know how we get one?"

Sage stopped pacing. "I have a couple friends in LA, but Haru, do you have any songs that might work?"

Haru shrugged. "Don't know if you guys would like it, but the title is 'I'm All Tied Up For You.'"

"Nice. Can you sing it for us?" Zen asked.

"'Course. The song can go big or stay soft and small." Haru did a run-through of the song and concluded with, "It's a bit rough."

"But the song is there. Polishing a few of the parts will be easy, though I'd be interested to hear the song both ways before we decide which direction we take it," Sage said.

Zen nodded in hearty agreement.

"I can release some photos on *Screaming Into the Void* Instagram account." Sage took the lead, which made Daiki's heart skip a few beats.

Wayuu hadn't moved.

"Then even if Ito releases it, people will assume the clip is part of the photo shoot." Haru sat back with a big grin.

"Would this even work?" Wayuu's words were filled with doubt.

Sage asked, "Why wouldn't it? And even if it doesn't, this band is about being who we are, not who people think we're supposed to be."

Wayuu's mouth dropped open, but he remained silent.

Zen leaned into Wayuu. "So you're into that?"

Blushing as if he were touching the sun, Wayuu pressed his lips together and shrugged.

"You guys really think this song will work?" Haru seemed shy for the first time ever.

"Yes, and if my vote counts, this could be a great way to brand our band." Zen looked around at each of the members.

"Sorry for being the cause of so much trouble." Wayuu's eyes watered.

Zen threw an arm around Wayuu and tugged him closer.

Sage stepped over to Wayuu. "We want to do this."

"It's what bands do," Haru stated.

Wayuu shook his head. "Fire didn't come together when there was trouble."

"Other than you, they weren't worth much." Patting Wayuu on the shoulder, Zen smiled.

"There's always going to be obstacles. Our job is to figure out ways around them. Where can we shoot this?" Sage asked.

Daiki couldn't sketch fast enough. When had he started drawing? "I know the owner of a club you could probably use. The premise in the manga could be that the band is at the party because of a lost bet, and… what?"

The band was staring at him. Daiki noticed because it changed how the moonlight made the shadows shift.

"Maybe. I mean, I can do any storyline…," Daiki backpedaled.

"You're perfect." Sage grinned at him.

Chapter 12

BY THE next morning, Sage, Daiki, and the band had reviewed the clip—Wayuu hid in the bedroom, claiming to be too embarrassed to watch with them—and Daiki had secured the use of the club. Sage FaceTimed with the twins from the venue.

"Any recommendations on how to shoot this space?"

"Other than to let me film it… nope." Lee was pissed.

Trying not to roll his eyes, Sage explained again, "I want it to look raw, not professional. Plus time is issue. We need these pictures immediately. But when we do more than promo shots, I'll ask for your schedule."

Ryder snuggled into Lee, and he seemed slightly mollified. "It's fine, Sage. Give us a tour. This club looks like a loft space or warehouse?"

"Upper floor of a warehouse. When you first walk in, it's a social area with tables and chairs and a few couches."

"What's the color scheme?"

Sage pushed the sheer curtains aside and directed his phone around the room. "Charcoal grays and black. Then there's an open play space with St. Andrew's crosses, benches and tables with restraints, several sex slings, a hospital bed, and a few flat surfaces. The owner said there are smaller rooms in the back, but I think it makes sense to shoot in the main area."

"The overall vibe appears to be abandoned warehouse with all concrete and metal beams," Ryder summed up the club's aesthetic.

"You doing any smoke?" Lee asked.

Sage tried to think about the clip he'd seen. "Not for this photo shoot, but I think for the video, yes? Smoke will lend to the fantasy of the forbidden."

"Absolutely." Lee's creative side kicking in evidently got him excited enough to forget he was pissed.

Sage wanted to bypass the idea of breaking taboos because it had been riding him hard all morning. "Anything else?"

Ryder gave him the now-famous smirk. "Add a touch more red to your lower lips."

Rolling his eyes again, Sage agreed, "Fine. Should I introduce you to the band?"

Lee's "Of course" was drowned out by Ryder's happy squee.

"Hey, guys, the twins want to meet you." Once the band was standing in a cluster, Sage directed the tiny camera at each one, said their names, and then said, "This is Ryder and Ryley."

Ryder started to mutter. "Holy fuckness."

Sage turned the phone to stare at Ryder and Lee. "What?"

"What? They're so hot dressed in all leather. Someone needs to lock them up, or maybe down…."

Sage glanced at his bandmates.

Zen smirked and continued to twirl a riding crop.

"Thanks," Haru called out while attaching cuffs to his belt loop.

Stepping back, Wayuu continued to stare at the floor as he touched the collar he wore.

They did look hot in BDSM gear, but Ryder didn't see what was truly sexy—Daiki in one of Sage's T-shirts, hunched over his sketch pad, totally enthralled by the lines he drew onto the page.

Lee kissed Ryder's head and purred, "You can lock me up as long as I have the keys to your heart."

When clearing his throat didn't stop the love fest, Sage said, "Okay. I'm off to do this photo shoot."

Ryder's laughter was deep. "We're off too… to get off. Later."

Lee said, "Later," and then yipped for a reason Sage was sure he didn't want to know about, right before the phone screen went black.

Zen asked, "Wait, are they related?"

"Everyone asks them that." Sage waved him off. "No, they're not."

Haru folded his arms over his chest. "Well, you did introduce them as 'the Twins.'"

"Everybody calls them that because they're inseparable. But they're not blood kin. As far as their relationship, you can ask them that when you meet them, but right now let's do this."

Wayuu glanced around the group. "Guys, I really appreciate you doing this, but I feel like it's asking too much. Don't you think it would be better if I left the band?"

"No." Zen was adamant.

"Better? Define that word." Haru questioned not only Wayuu's statement but his sanity.

For the umpteenth time, Wayuu seemed to be gearing up to discuss quitting. "It would be easier. That way you wouldn't be starting with such a risky first cut."

Sage's role would help them stay on track. "Kashi-sei means visibility. This isn't only about orientation or gender. This is about being you and expressing yourself. We're going to try to give validation to those who are different by stealing the stigma—"

"I should go. I—" Wayuu started to move toward the exit.

Zen grabbed Wayuu's wrist, stopping him.

"We can't force you, but we all want you to stay." Sage wouldn't apply pressure, but Zen looked like he was good doing whatever it took to keep Wayuu with them… him.

Wayuu groaned and combed his fingers through his hair with the hand not secured by Zen. "I feel terrible."

Haru leaned against one of the St. Andrew's crosses. "Hey, look at it this way. One of my songs may be the first Kashi-sei song released. That's huge for me."

Continuing to twirl the crop, Zen shrugged. "And hey, I've always wanted to know more about BDSM."

"Really?" Wayuu gasped.

Sage pressed his lips together so he didn't crack up. Hopefully these two would bring their chemistry to the stage. "So where should we begin?"

Daiki abandoned his sketch pad and appeared right next to him. "Um, there were kiss marks on Wayuu's neck that night. Should I try to make them?" He pointed at the makeup kit he carried.

Zen tilted his head. "Where were they exactly?"

Wayuu frowned. "I don't think you'd be able to—"

"But it makes sense to try to look similar to the clip." Sage pointed out the obvious.

"No need to fake anything. Where were they, Wayuu? Show me." Zen's glare directed at Sage was meant to be intimidating, and it was in stark contrast to the soft voice he used to try to mesmerize Wayuu.

"Right here and here." Wayuu tilted his head and identified the places on his neck.

Haru's laugh barked out. "Hey, Sage, why don't you have Daiki give you one too."

Yes! He'd like that, but Daiki seemed skittish about showing affection around others. "Um... Daiki?"

"How can I help you?" Daiki asked.

His lower voice sent tendrils of excitement through Sage. "Haru... thinks I should... you should—"

"Suck on his neck." Haru smirked.

Wayuu's moan seemed to echo off the cement walls. Zen had latched on to Wayuu's neck and walked him backward, only to be stopped by a wall.

Daiki stepped closer to him. "Do you want me to do this, Sage?"

He wanted Daiki's mark more than just about anything he could think of... and anything more he wanted involved Daiki too. "Yeah."

Running his fingertips over Sage's throat, Daiki traced the collar Sage had buckled around his neck earlier.

Sage wasn't really submissive, but he respected his need to surrender everything to Daiki.

Daiki caressed a spot on Sage's clavicle. "I'm going to mark you here."

Anticipation made Sage hard.

The bite probably wouldn't show, but that stopped being the point as soon as Daiki agreed to mark him... in public.

He groaned out, "Yes."

In a flash Sage tilted his head farther, and Daiki's tongue licked the target. Again and again, until Sage felt like he'd played a drum solo at the Super Bowl. Finally, Daiki scraped his teeth along Sage's collarbone and then sucked.

A shiver of satisfaction raced through him as Daiki pinched his teeth on Sage's neck and inhaled.

Daiki glided his lips closer to the collar and nipped with his teeth.

Sage pushed his fingers through Daiki's hair and pressed him closer.

Taking that as a request, Daiki sucked and bit and then sucked some more. Sage shifted to get his lower body some friction, and—

Haru cleared his throat. "I think you've got it."

Daiki stumbled away, but Sage couldn't let him go yet. He grabbed him and wanted to say so many things, but only "Thank you" came out.

Looking away, Daiki said, "You're welcome."

Their incredibly embarrassed but polite exchange made everything that much hotter for Sage. Daiki had marked him as taken. Happiness, contentment, and lust warred for top billing.

Sage planted a quick kiss on his mouth… in case those hickeys didn't make it clear who belonged to whom.

Wayuu wobbled his way over to the group with Zen steadying him. "How should we…?"

The husky timbre to Wayuu's voice told Sage he wasn't the only one affected.

Zen pointed across the room. "Wayuu, you were on the St. Andrew's cross. I'll help secure you to it. And as our other sub, Sage should to be tied to the spanking bench."

Everyone followed Zen's direction without question. Sage didn't know why he was surprised.

Haru arched an eyebrow in Zen's direction, but to Sage he said, "I understood the rules of branding and marketing, but Zen and Wayuu are both completely opposite of their previous public image."

Zen was dominant and direct but had appeared as compromising and needing direction. Wayuu used to strut around the stage like he owned it when, really, he wanted someone to tell him what to do.

Sage replied, "Not being themselves must have been exhausting."

"Would you like me to tie you to the bench?" Daiki's whisper filled in the blanks and gave Sage answers he didn't know he was searching for.

"Yes." Sage hoped his tone implied "without a fucking doubt." Shrugging off expectations freed and aroused him like nothing else ever had.

Daiki had a hand on Sage's lower back as he guided him over to the bench. He tugged Sage's hands to the premade cuffs. "Since this isn't a scene, you can simply put your hands through the loops and hold on."

Sage moaned and did as he was told.

"You like this, don't you?" Daiki's whisper made him so hot.

"You being in control and me surrendering in front of my band… I fucking love it." Sage turned his head to stare into Daiki's eyes.

"I think you like doing things that, somewhere along the line, you were taught you weren't supposed to do. It turns you on." Daiki outlined the basics Sage had barely admitted to himself.

"Yeah—fuck!" Daiki ripped Sage's T-shirt up the back, and the sexy action made Sage thrust his erection against the padding on the bench. How many others had been in this position and been spanked to orgasm?

Daiki pushed the torn fabric aside. He licked across Sage's angel wings tattoo.

Holy hell. Sage shoved his ass out in an attempt to contact any part of Daiki's body. Called out and spot-on. "Yes. Good."

Daiki pressed against him, giving him a reminder of his position. He nipped Sage's ear and whispered, "Good for me too."

Sage shook with need. A driving force for something, a need to come, a need for more, but most of all, his need for Daiki.

Haru paced between the cross and the bench. "Daiki, why don't you do the honors? I can take the pictures."

Sage swallowed hard. In the mirror in front of him, he could see the rest of the room.

Daiki picked up a paddle and caressed the wood. He peeked through his curtain of hair at Sage and gave him a tiny smile.

Oh damn!

Sage hadn't given BDSM a passing thought… not really. Yet having Daiki with the paddle tripped his switches. Pictures of Daiki hauling off and smacking Sage's ass became a throbbing drumbeat in his head.

Haru took photos.

He dragged his eyes off Daiki's reflection and suggested, "Maybe for the sake of realism, Zen and Daiki could actually, you know, connect."

Zen placed a hand on Wayuu's back. "I don't think that's necessary."

"Do it," Wayuu demanded breathlessly.

Sage looked over at Wayuu and decided a little sensation was what they both needed. Trying to keep his voice even was nearly impossible, but he was able to say, "Yeah, go ahead, Daiki."

The shock of the wood connecting to his ass reverberated through his body. Sharp pain eased into a hot sting that teased him.

The swat was echoed by Zen's paddle, and Wayuu hissed out a broken, "Ow."

"Too hard?" Zen's worried words reached Sage, pulling him back.

"*Ow* is not my safeword. Again, and harder." Wayuu's demand was clear.

Embracing what you needed was all kinds of hot. Sage thrust his ass out, hoping Daiki would continue too.

Smack! "Oh." The air rushed out of his lungs.

Smack! A burning sensation covered his butt and spread to his dick.

Smack! Sage let the wood push him against the bench, teasing.

Daiki rubbed the paddle against him, making him thrust back, begging for more.

Smack! Smack! Smack!

Oh God, yeah! Daiki gave it to him.

"Okay, that's great," Haru said.

Smack! Smack!

After clearing his throat, Haru assured them, "I got what we need."

Disappointment raced through Sage. It was over?

Daiki leaned into him. "One more?"

"Yeah." Sage loved Daiki was reading him so well.

And Daiki delivered the hardest smack yet.

"Ow." Sage was going to feel this into next week.

Daiki unlooped Sage's wrists from the ropes and helped him stand. "Come with me."

Zen snorted. "Only if you time it right."

Embarrassed but more turned-on than he'd ever been in his entire life, Sage allowed Daiki to drag him to privacy.

The lock clicked on the single bathroom.

"*Umpf.*" Sage was slammed against the wall. His heart skipped a beat at the unexpected act of aggression.

"You okay?" Daiki asked as he worked Sage's zipper down.

God, all the blood had left Sage's head. They had woken up late and hadn't had time for their usual morning orgasm, so he'd been hard for hours.

"No." Sage wasn't able to stop Daiki's fingers from opening his pants.

"No?" Daiki's question turned into a moan.

A kinky image of wearing Daiki became embedded in his brain. Sage unzipped Daiki's pants and then wrapped his hand around his erection. "I want more."

"Sage." Daiki's gasp only served to turn him on further, making his vision narrow until all he could see was Daiki.

The way Daiki said his name did things to him, inviting him to push the boundaries he'd always set for himself.

"Like that?" Sage spit in his hand to add an extra bit of glide to his twisting stroke.

"So hot. Before…. I never—oh, Sage."

Sage used his free hand to open Daiki's pants farther.

Daiki looked down. "Careful. I'm going to come."

"I know." Sage kissed him hard on the mouth.

When Daiki's lips parted, Sage chased Daiki's tongue with his own, then sucked his lower lip into his mouth. He released it with a nip.

"It'll be all over you." Daiki groaned between kisses they couldn't stop exchanging.

Some of the earliest fantasies Sage had ever had involved being coated, but he couldn't even entertain the idea with the men he'd been with. Safety first. But with Daiki—

"I want to be covered in you." Sage grazed his teeth along Daiki's neck, pulling a tortured moan from him before he kiss-sucked the area as he stroked him faster.

Daiki gripped his shoulder. He exhaled in a hiss as he unloaded warm spurts of cream all over Sage.

What a mind-breaking event. Cum shot all over him as his shaft throbbed with impatience.

He looked down at the mess he'd made. Kisses marked his neck and cum marked his erection.

"Mm, so filthy." A unique kind of horny power flashed through him, making him thirsty for more. Instead of acting on his desire, Sage stepped back; he needed to zip—

"Where are you going?" Daiki grabbed at his torn shirt.

Sage was turned-on but…. "I'm… they're right outside."

"I know." Daiki gave him a slow, sexy grin. He collected the cum that coated Sage with his fingers and ran it along Sage's needy shaft.

Swallowing hard, Sage rested an arm over Daiki's head. He couldn't take his gaze off the slow, teasing assault on his erection.

"I want you to stand here and know if you're too loud, your band will hear you." Daiki's evil smile called out all the filthiest parts of Sage, parts no one else had ever seen. Pieces of himself he couldn't even admit existed.

Sage gasped.

"Don't move," Daiki warned him.

He couldn't have shifted positions even if he'd wanted to, but Daiki's fingers gliding over him made being completely still impossible.

"I'm going to use my cum to jerk you to orgasm, but you better be quiet… or they'll hear." If the look in Daiki eyes was enough to ignite Sage's drumsticks, his hand wrapping around his shaft was enough to ignite Sage all over.

Daiki had taken control.

Sage loved how Daiki's cum eased the firm tugs, and he seemed to know exactly how to get Sage where he needed to be.

Spinning Sage around, Daiki pushed him into the wall. The sudden change in position charged Sage up even more. Everything in him coiled tight and built to this moment.

"Next time I'm not locking the door, and your band can watch me make you come."

Sage groaned.

"Maybe I can invite them in to watch me make you come right now."

The vision Daiki's words caused—oh God! Sage came… because he couldn't do anything else.

Daiki tugged him in time with the pulses of pleasure. When he was spent, Daiki's mouth caught his in the sweetest of kisses. From dirty to sugar in a matter of seconds.

"Here." Daiki grabbed the wet wipes off the shelf. "I think we should make a list."

"A list?" Sage's brains were on the floor with his cum. He could barely figure out how to get the wipes out of the packet.

"Allow me." Daiki opened the package and handed him one… and then another.

He was a mess. "Thanks."

"A Want-to-Try-It Sex List… and all the places we want to try them in." Daiki's voice was low, and he didn't quite meet Sage's gaze, but was he serious?

Sage's mouth dropped open, and he blinked in an attempt to clear his head. Daiki wanted to make a list of dirty sex things to try! "Am I dreaming?"

Daiki looked at the far wall and straightened himself. "No, I just think we share a similar interest that bears exploring… if you want."

Did he look stupid? "Oh, I want. I most definitely want."

Chapter 13

A COUPLE of weeks had flown by since he and Sage began compiling all things they wanted to try. This morning Daiki added oral sex on a train to their Want-to-Try-It Sex List. The possibility of being caught, while mortifying, was also titillating.

Daiki had never believed he'd ever find someone as filthy—eager to find pleasure in unique ways—as his characters, but Sage appeared ready to explore whatever... and wherever.

Their list might take years to accomplish, but that was quite all right with Daiki. The longer the better. Maybe it wasn't his characters who were needy, but him.

One of his assistants coughed. Right, he had a manga to draw.

Daiki pulled on the ears of his fox hat and growled. *Why isn't this working?*

"What?" Akihiro poked his head up from his workstation.

Oops!

The other assistants didn't stop laboring, but Daiki had their attention. "Something's not right with Kashi-sei's story."

"Want me to take a look?" Akihiro's cautious tone suggested Daiki might have been a bit possessive about the manga. When a new series was born, he was protective, but not letting anyone see even character sketches, let alone view the hashed-out storyboards, might have been overkill.

Daiki gave him a nod. He got away from his monitor and paced.

Akihiro glared at him. "Sensei?"

Sighing, Daiki backed away. "I'll be back."

He went into his room and packed a few more pairs of pants, his favorite jeans, and some more T-shirts. Daiki had been sleeping at the band's apartment every night. Things couldn't have been better if he drew it himself.

Last week, Sage stopped him from saying he was staying there to draw Kashi-sei. Sage encouraged him to admit Daiki was there to wake up next to Sage every morning. He tried to laugh it off by saying what man wouldn't want to wake up next to an orally fixated man.

But Sage denied him the escape by confessing he really liked Daiki… a lot. That admission was better than any round of oral sex he could imagine. Sage made him promise he'd bring a couple of personal items so Daiki could feel more at home in the apartment, since he was living there.

He was living with his boyfriend. The idea of cohabiting with a man had always seemed impossible, but here he was simply doing it. Maybe he should be missing his apartment or his life…. What life?

His location might have shifted, but his art still remained tightly wrapped around him. He did miss talking to Akihiro more often, so he found himself texting him, and they even had a few phone conversations. But there were so many positives to focus on—oral orgasms aside. Cuddling next to Sage and simply listening to him breathe eased Daiki to sleep; eating meals with him, sharing all the bits and pieces of life, and, most of all, having someone understand him more than anyone else, made up for any loss the move caused.

Daiki didn't know how this would all work out, but he couldn't stop smiling about it.

After a look around the room, he added a picture of his grandfather, one of his parents, who were working overseas, and a smaller canvas.

A knock at the door made him pause. "Yes?"

Akihiro poked his head into the bedroom. "Can we go up to the roof?"

That bad? "Of course. I could use some air." Daiki braced himself as they rode the elevator to the top floor. Sneaking peeks at Akihiro did nothing to reveal what the man was thinking.

Daiki jogged up the steps and took a deep breath as he stepped outside.

Akihiro didn't say anything but joined him at the railing and stared at the panoramic view of Tokyo. His apartment building was higher than most, affording a view farther than the next building.

Being up here usually gave him perspective, although right now impending doom loomed on the horizon.

"Tell me. What's wrong with the manga?" Time to rip off the Band-Aid. Usually characters were fragmented parts of himself mixing in with his wishes and dreams, so at times their intentions were garbled. The characters had always embodied shattered parts of himself he was too scared to be.

However, this manga was a presentation of real people. Guys he liked… and one he was pretty sure he loved. He didn't want to get it wrong.

"The storyboards are drawn beautifully." Akihiro was too diplomatic for Daiki's sanity.

"But?" He shoved his hands into his pockets. Anxiety streamed through him like the world had run out of paper.

Akihiro shrugged. "There is no struggle. The band fell into place and is working well. In the storyboards, there've been no arguments or drama in the practice sessions about the music. All the members agree on everything, even when making some pretty major decisions."

That's basically how it was. Daiki had counted the band lucky since they had many other challenges to face. But without the tension of an unfulfilled need, a risk with big consequences, or some other conflict, it became a day-in-the-life. "I see."

"The characters are interesting… fascinating, truly. I want to see, but everything in their world is flawless."

"Too perfect." Daiki's own feelings were bleeding over into the manga. Rookie mistake.

"Everything has been too easy. There need to be obstacles the band can overcome to give a sense of a satisfying conclusion."

Money did seem to remove many of the day-to-day problems, but it didn't solve everything. He needed to find something yen couldn't fix. "Got it."

Akihiro turned to him. "There must be some sort of struggle for them to work together to overcome."

Daiki nodded. There had been, of course, but Wayuu's problem wasn't for public consumption. "You're right. Where's the story? Clearly, future interactions with the fans, bleeding information into the storylines, but now… there's nothing."

"You'll find the story. It's there. And the work you've done thus far in terms of setting up the background gives an encompassing view of each member. Even after reviewing the BDSM party intro, I'm greedy for the band's adventures. I want more."

That made Daiki smile. Akihiro had never been overly generous with his praise. Daiki didn't remember Akihiro ever saying he wanted more of a particular story. Daiki'd find a way to make this right.

After a minute of silence, Akihiro finally asked, "I can't help but notice you're not sleeping here."

"Um… not recently." Why did Daiki hedge?

Akihiro tilted his head and observed him, making Daiki feel like a miniature painting Akihiro was studying with a magnifying glass. "You're living with him?"

Daiki nodded. There was no lying since Akihiro slept in the second bedroom more than Daiki had been in his own bed recently. His bed only seemed to be his if Sage was snuggled next to him.

"Do you love him?" Akihiro had a way of cutting through all the nonsense and honing in on the important things.

It hadn't been a gradual falling… more like an appearance of the first line on a storyboard. Each day more and more lines were added—along with vivid colors so bright at times it was blinding—and now he didn't know how to continue his own story without Sage. Though feeling that he was in charge of his own storyboards was good.

Again, Daiki didn't trust his voice, so he nodded.

Akihiro grinned. "Good. Sensei deserves to be happy."

"No warnings?" Daiki was surprised.

Staring out into the distance, Akihiro wore a ghost of a smile. "Don't let him go."

AKIHIRO'S *TOO-PERFECT* assessment of Kashi-sei's manga still bounced around Daiki's head as he stepped into the plush luxury apartment.

A track of the band's most recent practice session played. The lights of Tokyo twinkled through the balcony doors.

He set the painting and his bag down at the door and followed the sound of someone singing just a little off-key to the song.

Daiki rounded the corner to see Sage air-drumming around the kitchen as he got the dinner out of the delivery containers and into serving bowls. His longer hair was tied in front so the blond strands were out of his face but sticking straight up. The hairstyle made him look adorable, like an anime character.

Perfection.

Yes, Ikeda Daiki loved Sage Nakamura… there was no doubt.

Happiness seeped into every part of Daiki as affection splattered all over the storyboards in his mind.

But flawlessness couldn't go on forever. Perfection had an expiration date. He tried to brace himself because the storyboards his heart had drawn wouldn't allow him to hold back.

Sage did a fast riff on invisible drums and then spun around. He halted midbeat. One side of his mouth turned up in that sexy smirk of his that promised wonderful things would happen later tonight. The heat that quickly sketched between them in his brain seemed to wipe out Daiki's wish to capture this moment on the page, and instead he melted into Sage's open arms to burn the memory into both of their lips.

Daiki forgot all about storyboards, holding back, perfection expiring, and he just slipped deeper in love.

The pure satisfaction of finding the man he loved in the kitchen air-drumming… he'd never be able to draw that much joy.

Daiki's hands cupped Sage's face, allowing the smell of chicken rice bowls and a freshly showered Sage to become forever entwined in his mind with happiness.

Sage lowered his mouth to Daiki's. He glided his lips over Daiki's top lip and then his bottom lip. With patience and sweetness, his mouth covered Daiki's, making his lips part of their own accord to welcome Sage's tongue.

They playfully tangled their tongues, but then Sage walked Daiki back against the cabinet and friction happened. Sage ground his lower half against Daiki, causing need and desire to spill through him.

Sage nipped at Daiki's lower lip and then suggested, "Maybe dinner can wait a bit, and we—"

"Yes!" Zen howled, then yelled, "Yes!" again.

Daiki jumped back out of habit.

Sighing, Sage released him.

Three pairs of feet thundered toward the kitchen.

Zen clutched his phone above his head as if he were taking a victory lap. "We've got our first gig as Kashi-sei."

"What?" Sage stiffened like a ruler.

Not sure what made Sage look ill at the incredible news, Daiki rested a steadying hand on him.

Zen shifted from foot to foot, looking at them with anticipation.

Sage remained silent, so Daiki said, "That's great. Where?"

Haru rested a hand on Sage's shoulder. "Zen pulled in a favor. The Warehouse is letting us do a set."

"How did this happen?" Sage's tone made it sound like he wasn't aware playing music for an audience was high on their list of things to do as a band.

Zen shrugged. "I know it's a small club, only holds five to six hundred, but it'll give us audience feedback."

"Only?" Sage choked on the word. "Five to six hundred... people?"

Haru snorted. "Usually people make up an audience."

Daiki stepped closer to Sage, wishing he could help.

"Yeah, I wonder if we could create more of a buzz by making the show pseudo-secret," Wayuu chimed in.

Zen nodded and pointed at Wayuu. "I love that."

Haru stole a piece of chicken out of one of the bowls. "Usually bands that do that have a cult following. We don't have that."

"Not yet." Zen smirked.

"Aw, this guy. He's filled with confidence." Haru sneered and patted Zen on the back.

The three guys laughed.

Daiki dabbed the sweat off Sage's brow and whispered, "Are you okay?"

Sage made a strangled sound.

"Am I wrong?" Zen asked with the perfect amount of haughty idol mixed with hopefulness.

"Hey, two idols and a YouTube star in one band. I'm hanging on for the ride." There was truth in what Haru said.

Wayuu shook his head. "No need to downplay your talent."

Haru glanced around. "Did you see me do that? You guys have all sorts of expectations... whereas me? No one knows me."

Haru's bedroom door opened. "You're a hidden star who will go nova." All Daiki saw was a curtain of dark hair, and the door closed again.

Daiki had to ask. "Haru, is that your girlfriend?"

Haru's face was all aglow, making Daiki wish he could capture it on the page. "Yeah, she moved in late last night, and she's kind of shy. Ichi... Ichi, can you come out to say hi?"

The door reopened in slow motion and a young woman stepped out. She didn't make eye contact, but she waved.

Before she could disappear again, Haru pulled her to the group. "This is Tachibana Ichika. She is my heart, soul, and better half."

She bowed, greeted each of them, and told them to call her Ichika or Ichi.

Zen gave her his idol smile and asked, "How did you make the bad decision to hook up with our man Haru?"

Her gasp sounded more like a warrior call as she glared at Zen. "He's the best man I know."

Her bitten-out words seemed to force Zen backward. He held his hands out in front of him. "I'm just joking."

"Never tease about Haru not being the most incredible person in the world. It's incorrect and not amusing," Ichika warned, as if she'd go to war over another misstep.

Wayuu folded his arms over his chest and grinned. "I like you."

She turned her attention to Wayuu. Glancing up at his towering height, she nodded. "Thank you."

"Do you want some dinner?" Daiki asked.

"Thank you, Sensei, but I ate before I came back." She smiled at the group, except for Zen. "I appreciate no one having a problem with me staying with Haru."

"None whatsoever." Zen used his sweetest tone, as if trying to win her over.

She gave him a nod. "I'll go back to my work. Enjoy the night."

Everyone watched her head into the bedroom.

Zen patted Haru on the shoulder. "She's a tiger."

Haru smirked. "Just don't get on her wrong side. She does have claws."

Zen snorted but gave him a proud nod. "So I've noticed."

"I'm going to get some air." Sage stepped around the group and went to the balcony.

As soon as the balcony door slid shut, Wayuu, Haru, and Zen all stared at Daiki as if he had an answer.

Daiki had none so kept quiet.

Not being good with gray areas, Zen asked, "What's with him?"

"I don't know." Daiki hurriedly gathered the bowls and put them on the table.

Should Daiki go out there? Did Sage want to be alone? What should he do?

Zen shrugged and pushed a stack of plates and silverware to the middle of the table. "Maybe he's pissed I didn't ask him before scheduling the Warehouse."

"He doesn't seem like that." Haru grabbed out five beers and set them on the table.

Wayuu put a hand on Daiki's shoulder. "You should go talk to him."

Daiki went out onto the balcony. A rain drizzled down so lightly you couldn't see the mist unless you looked at the city lights at a certain angle.

Sage didn't even look at him. He kept staring at the skyline.

"What's upsetting you?" Daiki was working on being more direct, so he bypassed the usual back-and-forth.

"It's sudden. That show. Just all of a sudden, we're doing a show. It's out of order of our plan." Sage started drumming on the railing.

"But isn't this a good step? A small crowd to get some feedback." That's what Daiki thought the plan was.

"Small, yeah. Maybe that number isn't what those guys are used to but… that's a lot of people." Shaking his head, Sage continued to drum, a bit faster now.

Daiki was missing something.

"Why don't you go in and have something to eat. I'll be in soon," Sage said.

Daiki reached out, but Sage didn't respond. It almost felt like he was no longer in Daiki's storyboard, but that was nonsense. Daiki let his hand drop to his side. He'd give Sage some time.

As soon as Daiki stepped inside and slipped off his shoes, Zen appeared next to him.

"So? How is he?" Zen glanced out toward Sage.

Wayuu squinted out the windows to the balcony and then turned his attention to Daiki.

What could he say? "He's okay. Probably just needs some time to let everything sink in."

Haru nodded. "Yeah, that's it. It's a big thing Zen scored."

After a strained fifteen minutes of Daiki hoping everything would be okay, Sage joined them at the table. "Hey, sorry about that. Zen, great job."

"Why, thank you," Zen replied with extra bubble left over from his WTZ days.

Daiki filled Sage's plate.

"Thanks." Sage gave Daiki a smile that didn't reach his eyes.

It's okay. Everything will be fine. Sage is probably overwhelmed.

After four beers and only a few bites of dinner, Sage fell asleep on the sofa.

With Wayuu's help, Daiki got Sage into bed. "Thanks, Wayuu."

"Anytime. You really think it's all good?" Wayuu pressed his lips together and tilted his head toward the drunken Sage.

I don't know. I think so. I've never seen the man I've fallen in love with act like this.

Drawing on a believable smile, he gave Wayuu a nod. "Of course."

Wayuu shrugged. He didn't seem to buy it but adhered to the norms of agreeing. He left them alone.

Sage was already in sweatpants, so Daiki covered him with the blanket.

There would be no making good on the promises that kiss had made.

And just like that, perfection evaporated like paint left in the sun. Daiki could see the outline of the beautiful color, but he wasn't sure what to do with it.

Chapter 14

GLANCING OUT over the skyline of Tokyo, Sage wished he could see something other than his doom from the apartment's balcony. He tried to focus on the late-blooming sakura, but nothing eased the feeling or the tightening in his chest.

Zen opened the balcony door. "Mind if I join you?"

Nodding, Sage gave him a smile. Zen would be a great distraction as long as he didn't talk about the upcoming show. Wanting to ensure that, Sage asked, "Do you think the leaked photos of the BDSM shoot worked?"

Running his hands along the silver railing that ringed the balcony, Zen said, "Our social media platforms have been flooded with positives and appreciation. So I'd say it worked...."

Sage didn't miss Zen's concern. "What? Is Ito still harassing Wayuu?"

Zen shook his head with a frown. "Way says no."

"But you don't believe him?"

Shrugging, Zen tapped on the railing. "I'm not sure. Something is bothering him, and he's still worried, but isn't saying anything to protect the band."

"He should just tell the guy to fuck off." Sage didn't get how Wayuu seemed almost guilty for not bending to Ito's pressure.

Zen chuckled. "Easy for you to say."

"What do you mean?"

"If Wayuu's experience was anything like mine, the agency who managed him controlled everything. I felt dependent on them, and I was consumed with dread going against them even in the slightest way. I didn't want to disappoint them."

Only vaguely aware of the power dynamics that were sometimes used to control idols, Sage couldn't right the whole system, but he wanted to fix this one situation. "If it comes up, remind him I can front him the money owed to Ito. Whatever he needs. I've offered before, but—"

"I'll take care of him, though it's good to know you've got our backs." Zen patted him on the shoulder.

Sage could understand Wayuu not wanting to be beholden to anyone, but he wanted to help his bandmates in any way he could.

The silence had started to grow uncomfortable, and Sage reached for something to say. "So we're getting buzz on our platforms?"

"We are. But Way is getting too many offers." Zen gripped the railing and pulled upward.

"Offers of?"

Zen exhaled hard. "Idiots wanting to dominate him… have him dominate them, have sex with him… any number of inappropriate suggestions."

Sage tried to make light of it. "Maybe he'll find a Dom and—"

"Not out there he won't…. Have a good night." Zen stomped inside before Sage could respond.

Well, that was a distraction… though not a good one. Time to go inside.

Sage went into his—no, *their*—bedroom and found Daiki in bed, sketching. He locked the door and hoped tonight would be different.

Grinning, Daiki put his electronic drawing pad aside and spread his arms open wide. "Come here."

Straddling Daiki's lap, Sage cupped his face. He kissed him thoroughly.

Sexy Daiki was shirtless, willing, and all his for the taking… any way Sage wanted him, and yet again Sage couldn't. That perfect beat was just out of the reach of his drums… and dick.

As it had been for the last week, he couldn't rise to the occasion. His body felt out of sync with his need for Daiki. Sighing, he rolled off to the side of the bed and took Daiki into his arms.

Trying not to get into his head, Sage focused on Daiki, who throbbed and choked on moans for his attention. Sage pressed his lips against Daiki's and pushed the beast of worry away. He fumbled into Daiki's pants, wrapped his hand around Daiki, and then gave him a firm stroke. He used Daiki's foreskin to glide over the wet tip.

Sage whispered, "You're so hot." Daiki may not have had the experience most of Sage's past partners had, but he gave with such an open willingness that Sage's heart melted.

Rolling toward the middle of the bed, Daiki tried to get a grip on Sage's flaccid penis, but jumper cables couldn't put life into Sage. "I can—"

"I'm good," Sage shifted his hips away. He'd googled the hell out of erectile dysfunction.

The tests his parents insisted on before he moved to Japan ruled out most of the other medical possibilities, only leaving acute stress and anxiety to be the identified causes. If it didn't clear after the concert, he'd seek help from a physician because he didn't want to suffer with this for much longer.

He wished he could suck it up and get past the anxiety. There were so many things he and Daiki had put on their list, and he was more than ready to start checking things off—if only his body would cooperate.

But a dark cloud hung over him. The feeling of dread increased the closer the date Kashi-sei would play for an audience got.

An audience.... What had he been thinking?

A whimpering gasp drew Sage's full attention.

Daiki fanned his hand over Sage's body, and when he reached Sage's dead zone, he whispered, "You're more than good. I just want—"

"I'm stressed about the show." That was the understatement of the decade. Was he trading in his sex life for the band? No, this would ease up.

Daiki gave him a gentle look that broke Sage nearly as much as his insecure tone. "Maybe I could—"

Sage kissed him quiet. The doubt in Daiki's voice made Sage feel even more inadequate. As soon as Daiki relaxed in his arms, Sage pulled back from the kiss. "Things aren't working... right now. It's okay. Let me take care of you."

"But what about you?"

"I really like watching you... come." Sage did. Seeing Daiki fall apart in his arms was nothing short of magical.

Daiki writhed next to him as Sage stroked him to a quick orgasm.

"Sage," Daiki gasped as he came. He bit his lips as if he could stop the whimpering of release escaping from his sexy mouth.

When Daiki stopped shivering, Sage used Daiki's T-shirt to clean the sticky off them.

Gesturing toward Sage's problem area, Daiki said, "Don't you want me to try to—"

Fix my broken dick? "Nah, I'm good."

Daiki sighed but stopped with the fruitless suggestions, allowing Sage to pull him into his arms and absorb how good he felt there.

Daiki's eyes started to blink as he tried to stay awake.

Sage combed his fingers through Daiki's hair in a slow, steady rake that had Daiki yawning and then snoring in short order. He kept playing with the strands of Daiki's hair.

Five hundred wasn't a lot of people; after all, with any luck, Kashisei would be playing much bigger events.

He placed a hand over his chest. Wow, his heart was beating fast. How silly! His anxiety had dissipated while loving Daiki but now emerged stronger than ever. Sliding out of bed on max stealth, Sage made it all the way to the door.

"Sage?" Daiki sat upright in bed.

"Yeah?" Sage's hand froze on the door handle.

He turned. Daiki's covers pooled around his waist, his swollen mouth making him look all kinds of delicious.

"You'd tell me if there was something wrong between us... that if I wasn't making you happy, you'd say?" The words were said with a cautious calm, but Sage couldn't miss the worry that rendered each word rough with fear.

He rushed back to the bed and sat next to Daiki. Wrapping him in his arms, Sage said, "You are one of the few things that is holding me together. It's true I'm stressed, but I swear it has nothing to do with you or us. We're okay... right?"

Daiki seemed to hesitate for a long time as he stared at Sage. Finally he said, "On my end."

Sage needed to get himself together; otherwise he ran the risk of losing Daiki. "This show is really eating my brain. I'm sorry."

Daiki sighed. "Just tell me if I can do anything."

"I will." Sage wished he could lie down next to Daiki and sleep, but that wouldn't be happening. "I'm going to go to the music room for a while."

Nodding, Daiki grabbed his sketch pad off the nightstand. "I'll be here."

Sage wanted to stay with Daiki, but the worry drove him out. He made his way through the dark apartment to the music room. He flicked on the lights—too bright—then dimmed them and trudged over to his drums. He sat and twirled his sticks.

None of the usual calm found him as he spun the wood between his fingers.

How was he going to manage stepping out onto a stage in front of so many people? What had he been thinking? Maybe he should find another drummer to— No!

This was his dream. He wanted to do this… if only performing wasn't involved. He couldn't tell anyone else because it was crazy, right? One would think someone starting a band that wanted to give visibility and a voice to those who are different would have thought it through to the getting-on-stage part.

THE REST of the band was already on stage and in place doing sound check. Sage sucked on a peppermint Daiki had given him the last time he'd left the bathroom. The gesture removed any hope that Daiki didn't know any food Sage had ingested in the last year had left his system. He'd brush his teeth after sound check.

Ichika, Haru's girlfriend, gave him a worried smile and a thumbs-up. *I can do this.*

He nodded to her and tried to smile at Daiki like he hadn't just puked.

When that didn't quite work, he forced himself to step onto the stage. The too-bright room was loud, and their sound echoed. The studios he recorded in were contained and his drumbeat clear. How would the distortion affect their music? Okay, not at all, but this felt terribly wrong.

Then again, this room would be filled with people and all their noise. Even the most crowded studio control rooms had no more than five or six people. Oh God, how would he ever play?

"You okay?" Wayuu asked what the others were wondering, if their expressions were anything to go by.

Sage focused on breathing and tried to come up with the right answer. He took a couple more steps toward his drums, but his heart felt like a warning beat.

Stalking over to him, Wayuu was bigger than life on stage. He loomed over Sage and fussed with his shirt.

"What are you doing?" Sage stared down at how his T-shirt was now tucked in at the front and draped over his ass in the back.

As Wayuu rolled the sleeves of Sage's T-shirt, he said, "That's a french tuck."

Haru snorted. "Where did you learn about that?"

Wayuu pressed the now pristinely styled sleeves onto Sage's arms and gave him a smile. "The question is, how didn't any of you learn this?"

"'Cause I'm a musician, not a fashion model." Haru guided Sage over to his drums and gave him a bit of a push toward the chair.

Sage made his way behind his drums without falling, so he'd put that in the win column. Damn, he could see the entire venue… and it was a huge space.

Zen grinned. "Let's do the first song. Count us in, Sage."

The request should be simple, only Sage was having problems moving his hands.

"Sage?" Wayuu's concern cut through the anxiety.

"I'm good." What was the first song? "Um, 'I'm All Tied Up For You'?"

Zen nodded and made some adjustments on his mic. "Check. Check."

"I'm All Tied Up For You" was the song they were pairing with their BDSM photo shoot.

Wait, how did the song go?

Sage raised his sticks and tapped them together. Their beat was off, or rather he was, but he dragged himself through the song, avoiding the stares from his bandmates.

As he left the stage, Sage stumbled into Daiki's arms.

"Are you okay?" Daiki brushed the hair out of his eyes. He removed the band holding Sage's hair, finger-combed the wayward locks with gentle strokes, and reattached the band.

"Thanks. Much better." Sage dry heaved.

Daiki couldn't act unconcerned because his eyes had become cartoon circles. "I'll get you something to settle your stomach in a minute. First, let me hold you a bit longer."

Sage nodded because what could he say? Leaning into Daiki for a moment allowed Sage to absorb the warmth, but he failed to find any steadiness within himself.

Ichika held out a plastic bag to him. "Just in case."

Sage wanted to refuse but couldn't, so he nabbed the bag and thrust it into his pocket. "Thanks."

She backed away, probably to find Haru.

All too soon Daiki left for the Family Mart around the corner.

What could Sage do?

There would be no settling his stomach. He gripped his drumsticks tighter, hoping to stop his hands from shaking. His heart felt like it might beat out of his chest… and then he'd bleed out from not having a heart.

How can I go out on stage?

He wiped a hand over his forehead and then pulled at his T-shirt. "Why isn't the air turned on?"

Haru glanced up from his guitar. "It's freezing in here."

There was no way Sage could do this. He needed to put a stop to this.

It was only another thirty minutes until they needed to be onstage, but Sage couldn't hold the insanity in any longer.

"I can't do this." Sage stated a fact.

"Do what?" Zen asked.

Sage grabbed his stomach and tried to catch his breath.

"Clarify." Haru put a hand on Sage's shoulder.

"I'm not feeling well." Understatement of the year, but no sense adding drama. He could barely breathe.

Zen put a wrist to Sage's forehead. "You feel warm and clammy. Did you eat something bad?"

Could he pass this off as food poisoning? "I—"

"I heard you getting sick in the bathroom." Haru shrugged, and Wayuu nodded.

Great, everyone heard him puking his guts out. Sage popped another antacid, but he worried his body would rebel against even that. "We can't cancel."

"Okay, but you look terrible, so let's think." Zen started pacing. "I can synthesize the drums through my keyboard. I can keep the beat simple."

That shouldn't have hurt Sage, but it felt like a drumstick was driven into his heart. Of course Zen could, but he asked, "You sure?"

Zen put his hands on his hips. "Yup, fancy keyboard. We've got this, Sage."

Sage hoped that would be the case. "I'm really sorry."

He couldn't stay there another minute and burst out the back door and into the night.

Gasping for air, he inhaled. He exhaled. *Ahhhh.*

It felt like the first time air had filled his lungs and didn't have to push past dread and terror since Zen had scheduled the show.

Trudging to the front of the building while he practiced breathing brought him the reality. People had lined up around the block to see the show. Well, probably to see two used-to-be idols on one stage. Sage hurried away from the venue.

He should probably go back to the apartment, but instead he sidled into the first bar he came across.

After finding a quiet corner at the end of the bar, he ordered shots and kept flagging the bartender for more.

How cliché am I? Sitting at a bar getting plastered.

He rolled his drumsticks back and forth between two of his empty shot glasses.

The bartender had gotten into the bad habit of stealing the empty glasses, so Sage kept his fingers inside these two. Ha, he showed him who got to keep his shot glasses as drumstick stoppers.

These pieces of wood always brought him pleasure and peace, but for the last few weeks they'd brought nothing but anxiety and a limp dick.

Sage spun his phone in a circle. He'd powered it off. What a loser move.

He slammed back another shot. *Kanpai!*

Where was Daiki? He wanted Daiki. Right here and right—wow, he really did, but not just for some barroom sex, which, if it wasn't on the list, they could add it… but Daiki would know what to do.

Daiki was smart, kind, and everything lovely in the world.

How did he turn his phone back on?

The glass clunked against it.

Step one, take fingers out of shot glasses.

The device was slippery. He should cover it in sticky plastic. Oops! His cell clattered to the floor.

"That's bad." He laughed because he needed to slide off the stool and get his phone before someone stepped on it, but he didn't quite know how. The room seemed a bit off-kilter, but if his cell was crushed, how would he ever see Daiki again?

Oh no!

"Here. Let me help you." Daiki handed him the phone and stopped Sage from hitting the floor.

Happiness surged through him. "You. You appeared like an angel."

"This is yours. You're done drinking." The bartender handed Sage back his credit card.

"Well done, sober self." Sage grinned, or at least he thought his mouth was in the right position. "Thanks."

Was he slurring?

He turned to see Daiki's concerned smile—yeah, he was slurring. "Don't want to go back to the apartment, Daiki."

"I know of a place nearby."

"Lead on." Sage threw an arm around Daiki, and things started to feel okay again.

Chapter 15

"ARGH! DAIKI... we've walked forever." Sage exhaled loudly in Daiki's ear for the seventh time in the past thirty seconds.

"Careful, Sage." Daiki steered his rather drunken boyfriend around some debris caused by the area construction.

"Yes, Sensei." Sage sounded beleaguered but willing to continue to march across Japan the long way if Daiki asked.

Daiki bit back a smile. A drunk Sage was an adorable Sage... but then again so was a sober Sage. "We're almost there."

He had guided Sage up the incline, past the various hotels, and now they were on the other side. Less construction meant fewer ditches for Sage to fall into.

Sage's head popped off Daiki's shoulder. He stopped and looked around. A moment of clarity could be read in his expression. "Wait, is this Love Hill? Are you taking me to a no-tell motel?"

"What's that?"

All of Sage's usual cool escaped with his snort. "Isn't this where people come to do the naughty?"

"The naughty?" Somehow Sage had morphed into one of Daiki's adolescent characters, which didn't bode well for informed consent to do anything at a hotel other than sleep.

"You know... I haven't been, shall we say, in the mood with the stress of the.... How did I not know I had stage flight?" Sage had stopped slurring, but now he wasn't using the right words.

"You mean stage fright?"

"No. I mean I saw the stage and fled." Sage laughed. "It's bad, but I'm so glad I'm not on that stage right now."

Daiki didn't want to ask more, but he hoped Sage would fill in the blanks.

"On my YouTube channel, I have lots of views, but it's only after I have time for edits, and then I can shoot again and again as often as I need."

Lines that Sage had slashed onto his storyboard hadn't made sense, but now the lines were forming a picture so Daiki understood the truth. "And there are no redos on the stage."

Sage stared at him. "Exactly. You screw up on stage and you can't go edit that out. Your mistake will live forever. To be mocked and made fun of on a loop and in memes by all the haters."

"Mm." Daiki nodded. "I'd find it terrifying if someone were to see my first storyboards."

"Yeah?"

"Most definitely." At Daiki's urging, they began walking again. Sage wasn't staggering as much, but he wasn't walking a straight line either.

"Here we are." Daiki maneuvered him into the private, dimly lit lobby of a hotel. He tapped on the screen of an automated check-in machine a few times, and a key card dropped out.

Sage air-drummed but then turned and became distracted by the drinks and food laid out on a table. He grabbed a tray and slid a number of complimentary Saran-covered dishes of sandwiches, cakes, puddings, and candies onto it, along with a teapot, cups, and tea.

"You must be hungry." Daiki grabbed a couple of bottles of cold water. He was delighted, since Sage hadn't been eating much and what he had hadn't stayed in him long.

On the way to the elevator, Sage ate several cookies and stuffed one into Daiki's mouth. They got off on the second floor and entered their room.

The windowless room was tinted the color of pink sorbet, and the thick bedding had dark magenta roses on it. The matching canopy and the fluffy pillows called to mind a princess bed of eighth-grader fantasies.

"So do you come here a lot?" Sage's arched eyebrow suggested irritated jealousy.

The heater kicked on, humming and breaking into the silence. After Daiki swallowed the cookie, he said, "I've never come here."

"Yet… but you will. I'd better put this down… unless you'd *like* me to hold it?"

Daiki forced himself not to remember the details of that wild morning when he'd simply acted on his instincts. No, this was a time to use his brain. He smiled and said, "You can set it down."

Setting the tray on the bed, Sage gave him a saucy wink. He appeared somewhat steadier on his feet.

Sage lunged toward Daiki and latched on to his neck in the most delicious way.

Good as his mouth felt, Daiki gently pushed him back. "You're drunk and hungry."

Sage glared but weaved his way over to the bed. He inhaled several other treats as he drunk-dialed the TV remote. Then he turned off the TV and tossed the remote into a chair. "I'm horny and feel stupid."

"Why do you feel stupid?"

He groaned. "How could I not know I'd freak out about going on stage?"

Daiki froze the image into his mind's storyboard. Sage—eyes huge and head shaking—sitting in the middle of a big pink bed with frilly pillows behind him.

He sat beside Sage on the bed and squeezed his shoulder. "You never had the experience, so it's not surprising that you didn't know your reaction to it."

"I guess." Sage pulled the band from his hair, letting the bleached-blond waves free. "So how do you know about this place?"

Daiki's face heated. Why should he be embarrassed? Coming to a love hotel alone... "I needed to do research for a story. I reserved a room nearby, but this hotel looked nicer."

"Who did you come here with?" Sage picked nonexistent lint off the bedding.

"No one." Daiki's voice squeaked like he was lying, but it was actually surprise at the jealousy reappearing in Sage's tone.

"Really?"

Daiki didn't respond other than to tilt his head. Just him and his right hand... and a few drawings.

"Right. Sorry. Um, good." Sage did a quick roll with more coordination than Daiki expected him to have and put Daiki on his back with Sage straddling his middle.

"What are you doing?" Daiki's hands were being held pinned above his head in a very interesting way.

"I know we've not been together much lately, but I hope I still remember how to put the moves on you." Sage gave him a smirk that could have made every uke in Daiki's head squee, and then he shifted his butt right over Daiki's—

With care Daiki pushed Sage over to the other side of the bed and sat upright.

Sage scrunched up his nose. "Isn't that why you brought me here?"

Shaking his head, Daiki reminded him, "You said you didn't want to go to the apartment."

"Oh, well, right, but we can still—"

"Why don't we sleep for a couple of hours." Consent mattered, and someone who was as drunk as Sage appeared couldn't give consent, even if his body seemed very interested.

"Why don't we sleep afterward—"

Daiki rolled off the bed and stood next to it. "One of the educational pieces I'm going to work into one of my mangas is nonconsent and dubious consent. Both were hot back in the day, but now we know better, so we need to do better."

"But we're together. I'm giving you consent...." Sage undid his jeans and tried to push them off his hips.

"I'll tell you what. We have twelve hours here. Let's get some sleep, and then we can try something on our list." Daiki stifled a chuckle.

Sage failed to hide a sugar-crash-induced yawn that dimmed the sparkle of excitement in his eyes. "Can we get more time?"

Not sure why they'd need it, Daiki asked, "Twelve hours isn't enough?"

Sage snorted. "Just, you know, asking...."

Daiki grinned. "Yes, of course. There's a machine by the door. We simply insert a credit card and—"

Sage started snoring.

As Daiki quickly undressed Sage down to his purple silk briefs, he congratulated himself for making the right decision.

He finger-combed Sage's hair out of his eyes and tucked the duvet around him.

Checking out the rest of the room, he found a huge bathroom with every body- and skin-care product he could think of and a large Jacuzzi tub with many attachments. He took a long bath and utilized everything until he was squeaky clean.

After wrapping himself in one of the plush robes provided, he took his electronic drawing tablet out his messenger bag and did a few studies of Sage sleeping—with his arm thrown over his head, his shirt off, and the covers hiding the fact he still had on his underwear.

Daiki had to shake himself. If this was what happened when one took risks, why hadn't he taken any before? His heart answered, *Because there hasn't been anyone worth making mistakes with.*

Could he actually be landing exactly where he'd always wanted to be?

He set aside his sketching device and slid under the covers.

Sage murmured in his sleep and wrapped his arms around Daiki, sending love and affection cascading through him. This couldn't have been better if he'd drawn it himself.

BREATH TICKLED his nose. Daiki opened his eyes and found Sage smiling at nose-touching range. Rolling from his side onto his back, Daiki asked, "How are you feeling?"

Sage thrust his lower half against Daiki's thigh. "Better. Much, much better."

Daiki chuckled at Sage's smirk. "I'm glad."

"I might have been drunk last night, but didn't you mention working on our list?" Sage certainly knew how to turn on the sexy.

"Did I? I thought that might have been you." Daiki escaped into the bathroom to deal with life and brush his teeth.

Sage followed him.

Their now-familiar domestic ritual morphed into the sensual because Sage kept touching him. Little grazes as he reached for the second toothbrush. He changed Daiki's plan of a quick shower into something else entirely when he stepped behind the glass and massaged Daiki's body with soap until Daiki panted for more.

The feeling of Sage's lips on the sensitive parts of Daiki's ear almost made Daiki miss Sage asking, "What was the last thing you added to the list?"

Excitement and embarrassment coursed through Daiki in equal measure. "Oral sex on a train."

"Hot. Seems like we both have a fetish for the taboo—"

"You don't think it's weird?" The truth was Daiki wanted to do everything he'd drawn once, and then a second time to make sure he did it right.

"No."

He studied Sage. *Is he serious?*

"I don't think either of us wants to get dressed, but maybe we can practice right here." Sage tossed him a towel. Once they had dried off, they hung the damp towels back on the rack, put on the robes, and then Daiki trailed after Sage into the bedroom.

Sage had an artistically beautiful face and body, not just because of his muscular upper torso. He was well put together, but it was all the little things. The waves in his sexy bleached-blond hair when he let it loose. That sexy twitch his mouth made before he smirked. Oh, Sage's lips expressed so many things, sometimes all at once. He quirked them playfully, smirked in a sexy, nonarrogant but knowing way, and gave heartwarming smiles. So many lovely smiles Daiki could draw—

Oral sex on the train—Daiki pressed Sage against the dresser so he leaned back.

Sage gasped the way he had at the BDSM club when Daiki put him against the bench. "Tell me what you'd do to me on the train."

Swallowing hard, Daiki found the courage to tell him. "The train would lurch. I'd lose my grip on the grab triangles. I'd fall to the floor."

"Is the floor dirty?"

Daiki dropped to his knees and untied Sage's robe. He parted the fabric and caressed Sage's thighs. Sage's broken moan pushed an undeniable power straight through Daiki. He felt like he could do anything. "Filthy."

Sage shifted his body, causing the tip of his shaft to poke out of his robe and brush across Daiki's lower lip.

"May I?" Daiki's voice had gone rough and husky.

Sage gave him an "I plan to fuck you up against the wall, but I can be patient" smile. He arched an eyebrow and asked, "Is the train empty?"

Daiki stopped himself from looking away. He wanted to be bold, so he gave Sage a casual shrug that said he didn't care one way or another. "Probably not... it's rush hour."

Sage gripped the edge of the dresser, turning his knuckles white. The tip of his shaft was glistening with a droplet. "What's next? I don't think I can—"

"I'd unzip your jeans, pull your big cock out where anyone might see it, and suck you. Suck you right here in front of everyone." Daiki usually only wrote those words to hear them....

Sage groaned. "Daiki, it's been a while."

Daiki swiped his tongue across the tip of Sage's penis and took the sweetness from him. The robe slipped off Sage's shoulders and fell to the floor.

"This isn't going to take long." Sage trembled.

Enough teasing. Daiki wrapped a hand around Sage's base and stroked him into his mouth. He rocked as if he were on a train.

They would probably never do this on a train, at least not in Japan, but right now the fantasy was good enough.

"I've missed you in my mouth." He french-kissed Sage's erection around the words. He sucked him inside and bobbed his head.

"Coming." Sage grunted and came.

That was fast. Keeping pace with the pulses Sage unleashed in his mouth wasn't possible, but Daiki did his best.

When Sage finally stopped shaking and coming, he didn't go soft or get overly sensitive. He seemed ready for more, so Daiki kept licking him.

"Quicker than I expected. Come here." Sage pulled him off his knees and up to his lips and kissed him. He didn't seem to care that he had filled Daiki's mouth with his cum.

Hot, wet kisses gave Daiki an electric kind of need.

Rocking against Sage caused friction to spark through Daiki, making him want more.

Sage bit his bottom lip and then pulled back. "You know what I've never really tried but I want to?"

"What? I'll try anything with you." Did Daiki say that? He'd have to work on his uke dialogue, but no truer vow had ever been made.

"Can I rim you?" Sage's skimmed his hands inside the robe and palmed his butt.

"Rim me?" Daiki ran through what that would entail. Sage's tongue and his... his ass would be involved.

"Yeah. I've never wanted to do that, but I really want to try it with you... and then...."

Daiki needed clarification. There were too many possibilities dangling out there. "And then what?"

"Well, I mean, only if you're up for it... maybe after, I could be inside you?" Sage picked up one of the hotel-brand lubed condoms and the bottle of lubricant. He shook them in front of Daiki with a winning smile.

"Oh...." He'd never done either of those things.

Sage shook his head. "We don't have to. I thought—"

"No, I want to... I just... I've never, but I'd really like to." Daiki reached for what he wanted. He spun around and faced the mirror, ensuring that Sage understood he was serious.

Sage slid Daiki's robe to the floor to join his own.

Within a hot second, Sage had dropped to his knees behind Daiki, and the delicious yet disturbing sensation of Sage's tongue swiping across his ass commenced. He painted wet patterns over one cheek and then the other. Ever so slowly, he edged closer to Daiki's hole but always veered off at the last second.

Over and over, again and again, Sage's tongue avoided where Daiki needed him the most.

The insanity of the moment made him want to part his cheeks and guide Sage to where he ached. He leaned forward to give Sage a formal invitation. He'd drawn this plenty of times. The itch... a need... something he'd not quite experienced before, and Sage's tongue—

"Ahhhhh, yes." Daiki gasped and thrust back. All pretense of modesty or decorum had fled the storyboard.

Sage said he'd never done this, but he parted Daiki's ass, arrowed his tongue, and darted in and out of Daiki's crevice. He must be a quick learner, because he appeared to be an expert at it.

"Deeper." Daiki needed so much more. He thrust his hips back farther to encourage Sage.

Sage cupped the sides of Daiki's ass and pulled him closer. He pressed his tongue in farther and licked, ripping another shameless moan from Daiki.

He didn't care. His total focus was on getting more of what he craved... Sage. Everything in Daiki reached for something just out of—

Glancing at the mirror, he froze.

This was a drawing he didn't recognize. His face was wet with perspiration, his hair every which way, his eyes half-closed, and his mouth gaping, trying to drag in air.

And all he wanted was more. Daiki trembled as he spread his ass, thrusting back yet again to chase the pleasure.

The storyboard of reality—the mirror—didn't lie. Sage had somehow magically evolved Daiki into the very picture of outright need.

Daiki was shocked but too turned-on to put an end to this any other way than by begging Sage for mercy. "Please, Sage."

After a few more glorious minutes, hours, or years, Sage kissed along Daiki's spine, taking too long to appear over his shoulder. "You sure?"

"Very." He had to have Sage in him to replace the emptiness. The open space wasn't in his body alone but in his heart, mind, and soul. "Please fill me. Please—"

Gentle fingers found their way inside him, making Daiki wonder if this was a good idea. After a few twisting thrusts, Sage nudged his prostate, and Daiki pushed back, whimpering.

"Shhh, I've got you." Sage added more lube inside Daiki and put on a condom.

Daiki braced himself as he stared at Sage's reflection. Their gazes locked, sharing this moment caught between rush and forever.

With too much care, Sage inched inside of him.

Daiki shifted right and then left. There didn't seem to be enough room, but then Daiki's muscles relaxed and let Sage push past them.

Sage's eyes widened. "I won't last long."

"Doesn't matter. This is ours." Maybe that was not a bad thing for Daiki's first time. He gasped for breath, feeling way too stretched. Daiki tilted his head back.

Leaning forward, Sage froze except for his lips, which caressed along Daiki's neck.

Need licked through Daiki, making him restless for more.

"So good. Take what you want." Sage pressed against him. He took two slow steps back to the bed and sat with Daiki on his lap.

Daiki glanced over his shoulder. "What should I—"

Sage shifted and nodded toward the mirror. "Stay with me. Move if you can."

Complying, Daiki stared at their reflection. "How should I—"

Sage wrapped a hand around his shoulder, put the other under his butt, and helped him slide up and then back down.

Daiki bit his lip but groaned anyway.

"I'm yours. Take what you need." Sage's words wedged in between his heart and soul, painting them the color of love.

Daiki shifted his hips, and the delicious pressure zipped through him. His body forced him to glide forward and back.

"Yes. Good." Sage's praise embarrassed him because he needed it.

Daiki made to stand but sat before he disconnected from Sage. Again and again, he rode him, until his legs started to shake.

Sage got the message and supported his weight with both hands as he directed his attention on that special spot.

"Sage?" Daiki felt the beginning of an orgasm. He reached back and grabbed Sage's shoulder to tug him closer. He waited, but instead of ejaculating, he just hovered in a scorching hot pleasure zone. Moaning and shaking, he tried to piece together what was happening to him.

"So hot. Go with it," Sage whispered as Daiki clung to him.

There wasn't anything else Daiki could do. He was being overwhelmed by an intense rapture.

Sage thrust into him, and Daiki twisted forward and put his hands on his knees. He struggled to hold on as the pleasure kept echoing through his body.

"Fuck," Sage groaned and grabbed on to Daiki's shoulders, moving him a bit faster. Then he stiffened and grunted.

There was no controlling any of this, and that made it even more perfect. Soul-stealing ecstasy nailed him, but he didn't ejaculate, though he felt like he had come. Had he even been hard?

The grip on his shoulders lightened, and Sage glided him slower until he stopped moving him.

Sitting on Sage's lap, Daiki continued to study their reflection. He was connected to Sage physically, emotionally, and now, it seemed, spiritually.

Sage helped him to a standing position and slipped out of him but stood close behind him, giving Daiki a place to lean.

A gaping want tried to swallow Daiki, but Sage held him, bringing him gradually back to equilibrium.

What now? They'd just had intercourse. Daiki had taken Sage into his body and… how would he draw this?

"Let's take a bath." Daiki went full-on uke and filled the tub with lavender bubbles. He turned on the jets and stepped into the shower briefly to wash the lube out of him.

Sage moaned as he sank into the warm bubbles. Now there was a storyboard. Before Daiki could get paper and pencil, Sage reached his hand out to him.

Daiki grabbed the offered hand and stepped into the tub. He lowered himself into the warm water and leaned against Sage's front.

Sage wrapped his arms around Daiki. He massaged Daiki's shoulders, chasing away any remaining tension.

"That's good," Daiki said.

"Is this better?" Sage's hands skimmed down his wet chest and plunged under the water. He teased Daiki forever until he was erect.

Somewhere along the way, he decided the attention of Sage's hand was very much better.

Groaning, Daiki thrust into Sage's hand.

"Enough time has passed. Sometimes, when the prostate is involved, your erection can fade into the background." Sage's words were calm and controlled; Daiki's brain did a backflip.

One of his assistants had talked about how most people believe male ejaculation and orgasm are the same thing, but she proudly announced they were two separate things. Now Daiki had experienced exactly what she meant.

Daiki lay back farther onto Sage's chest, giving him access to everything he wanted access to.

"You were sexy before, coming on my cock." Sage captured Daiki's mouth in a kiss that pushed him over.

Daiki arched his back as waves of pleasure started in his core and thundered outward. He came hard.

Sage added hot water, waking Daiki out of his stupor. "That was…."

"Yeah?" Sage eased him over to the other side of the tub and then grabbed a foot and started kneading the sole. "I wanted everything to be good for you."

"Incredible." Daiki, boneless but determined, followed suit and rubbed one of Sage's feet.

Sage's crooked smile was filled with pride and happiness. It could have competed with the sun if they hadn't been in a windowless bathroom.

A FEW orgasms later, as Daiki toyed with Sage's hair, he noticed the time. "Our twelve hours is over in thirty minutes."

Sage made a show of peeking under the covers. "I don't think either of us will be getting it up anytime soon."

Daiki snorted. "The things you say. Sometimes I remember how American you are."

"What? Am I wrong? Granted, I had been a bit pent-up, but... not no more. My man done drained me," Sage teased.

His purposefully awkward grammar made Daiki wrap his arms around him. He never wanted this feeling of freedom and love to end. "You're silly, but amazing."

Sage raked his fingers through the disaster that was Daiki's hair and came back with "That's what he said. That's a joke from—"

"I know. *The Office*... but do you want me to add more time to the room?" Daiki rolled off the bed to find his credit card.

"Nah, but I don't want to go back to the apartment yet. I need time to figure everything out."

Daiki shouldn't have just assumed Sage would want him included. "Oh, should I leave—"

"Please stay. I need your advice and help thinking this through. You know, if you don't mind."

Feeling too many things, Daiki gave him a nod. He opened the cabinet containing clothing for purchase so he didn't do an embarrassing happy dance.

He gathered underwear, socks, and T-shirts for both of them. "Let's take a shower and head out."

"Where to?"

"I've got a place I go when I need to think. There's plenty of shops on the way to the station where we can pick up clothing." Daiki tried to remember the train schedule.

"We're going on a trip?"

Chapter 16

THE BUILDINGS of Tokyo got farther away as the train heading to Kyoto tracked through smaller towns.

Sage needed to suck it up and call the band. They had to be pissed at him for abandoning them last night. There were signs about no cell phones, but none in their first-class car. Their railway carriage was oddly empty.

Turning to Daiki, Sage waved his cell. "Since no one's in here, do you think it'd be terrible if call the guys?"

Daiki continued to stare at the window but gave his hand a squeeze. "Usually I follow all the rules, but I'm questioning that philosophy. There's no one you'd be disturbing, so I have no issue."

Sage dialed, and FaceTime connected him with Zen.

"You okay?" Zen asked, full of concern.

"Yeah. I'm sorry, man. Can you get the guys together?" Sage didn't want to do this, but if he had to, he only wanted to spill his guts once.

Wayuu appeared in the screen instantly alongside Zen.

The way the picture jiggled, they were walking, and then Zen knocked on Haru's door. He knocked again, harder this time.

Wayuu scrunched his face. "*Tsk*, we're sorry to bother you both."

"Haru! Haru! Get your ass out here. Sage is on FaceTime." Zen was more direct.

There was a thud and "Butterscotch... no, wait." Haru appeared, pulling on a shirt and panting.

"Butterscotch?" Zen snorted.

Haru glared. "A conversation for another time."

"Oh, most definitely, *Butterscotch*." Zen's eyes sparkled like "another time" would be directly after this discussion.

Sage forced himself to begin. "First let me say, I'm truly sorry. I let you all down."

"Hey, it worked out. The audience loved us," Zen claimed.

"Yeah, they really did." Haru sounded a bit shell-shocked by his own words.

Maybe this would all be for the best. Kashi-sei didn't need him. Each of them was taking a risky career move by joining the band. They didn't need a flake screwing them up. Finding another drummer wouldn't be hard. "I'm going to start looking for a new drummer. I can—"

"No!" All three of them shouted at him.

In the window's reflection, Daiki's mouth opened and then closed. Sage wished he'd spoken, but maybe this was something Daiki thought Kashi-sei needed to hash out.

Sage nodded in understanding. "Would you rather keep the band with you three? That's okay. I can—"

"What, you think you can quit?" Zen raised his voice to cutting level as he glared into the phone.

Sage held the phone farther away. "Look, I appreciate it, but I don't think—"

Wayuu cut him off. "Sage, I've never worked with a drummer who cares more about the music and highlighting others than he does about showing off."

In truth, Sage did solos on his channel to appease his fans or to make a point. He really didn't like the spotlight, but he enjoyed helping direct the listener to the music and other members.

Them wanting him to stay was an ego stroke, though he needed to be realistic if the band had a chance of succeeding. "You deserve a drummer who isn't dealing with... with stage fright."

"Oh, is that all it is. *Pfft.*" Haru folded his arms over his chest.

Zen laughed and then rolled his eyes. "Man, I thought it was serious."

"It is serious. What part of 'I would have chosen death rather than taking the stage last night' do you not understand?" Okay, maybe not quite, but damned close.

"I jump up and down in place," Wayuu stated, like that habit should make sense to Sage.

Haru tapped his forehead. "Oh, that's what you were doing. I thought... never mind. I run through all the chords of the songs in the set."

"I fuck," Zen said in that deadpan way of his.

Wayuu turned and glared at Zen. "What?"

Snorting, Haru said, "I'm going to tell my girlfriend I've got a new technique to ease preshow jitters."

A muffled "I wouldn't advise it if you want to keep her" drifted through Haru's door.

Zen looked at the two standing next to him and then back at the screen. "A question I never thought to ask—did you ever perform in front of a live audience?"

"No… well, one disastrous performance in high school." Sage couldn't stop berating himself for being so arrogant as to think he could simply take the stage.

"Ahhhh." Wayuu smiled in that reassuring way of his.

"Though I just identified that as problem number one. Millions of views on YouTube doesn't translate to the stage."

"We'll figure this out," Haru said with such confidence Sage almost believed him.

Wayuu squinted. "Are you on a train?"

"Yeah, heading to Kyoto, then on to Inari with Daiki—"

"Ohhhhh, nice." Zen smirked and leered.

A sliver of guilt weaved through Sage. "I'm going to take some time to figure this out. I'll be back in a couple of days."

"Have fun." Zen made riding a train sound extremely dirty.

"We'll be here, and be clear we are keeping you as the drummer of Kashi-sei." Wayuu did an air rim shot and waved.

"Seconded. Later." Haru gave a nod.

"Now, Butterscotch, where are you going?" Zen chortled as Haru disappeared and his door slammed shut. Zen grinned into the phone. "I'd tell you not to do anything I wouldn't, but there's not much I wouldn't do, so I'll say have fun."

"Take care." Sage ended the call, feeling much lighter but still confused.

Daiki grinned at him. "I'm glad Kashi-sei isn't going to allow you to escape… and neither am I."

As he and Daiki meandered the short distance through the town right below the Inari shrine, Sage thought out loud, "I've lived in LA most of my life, so I drive everywhere. But even connecting to the other train was simple."

"I'm sure there might be times a car would come in handy, though I can't imagine driving everywhere." Daiki led him past the souvenir shops, traditional tea shops, and a number of tiny restaurants that lined the road leading to the shrine.

Sage snorted. "That's because you'd have to put down your sketch pad. I'd have to make No Drawing and Driving billboards for you."

Daiki laughed and leaned into him. "I always put down my sketch pad to hold your hand."

Grabbing Daiki's hand, he gave it a squeeze. He stopped and took a picture of the manhole cover with an artistically drawn fox on the top. "Kitsune?"

Daiki's smile made him glad he'd remembered a bit of the information from his first trip here. "Yes. They're messengers pleading to the gods on behalf of the worshippers."

Sage read the plaque and then asked, "So all the offerings are for prosperity in business? Kashi-sei could use some luck."

Daiki nodded and led him to the start of the path. "Maybe in the future Kashi-sei can add to the 10,000 torii gates."

A lump formed in Sage's throat. He didn't want to give up being the drummer of his dream band, but he couldn't see the solution.

Catching on right away, Daiki threw an arm around him. "Hey, like the band said, we'll figure this out."

That *we* made the lump impossible to swallow past. He smiled at Daiki.

Daiki patted him on the back and released his hold. "Sometimes setting the situation aside can help a solution appear."

Pressing his lips together, Sage avoided his insecurities spurting everywhere and so nodded. "Some might say that's avoidance."

"Your American is showing. It's okay to coexist with a problem. Think of this as taking the time to see the issue from every angle."

"All I see is stage fright blocking me from performing." Sage was frustrated and angry and—

"You might be too close to the problem. Let's enjoy the walk up to the top. Let the Inari help you." Daiki gestured for him to start on the steps under the scarlet gates that lined the path.

Maybe it made sense just staying in the present moment. Sage took a big inhale and started moving on the exhale. "Being out of the congestion of LA and Tokyo is great."

"The walk is about five kilometers up and down through the torii gates. Want me to carry the pack?" Daiki asked.

"I've got it." Sage readjusted the straps. The knapsack wasn't heavy. It only carried a couple of sets of clothing for each of them, charging cords, and some protein bars.

"I'll hold the water." Daiki put the two bottles they'd gotten before leaving the station in his ever-present messenger bag.

Sage might have been joking when he asked, "What color red is this?"

However, Daiki the artist smiled at him. "Vermillion. The color used to be made from powdered cinnabar."

"Oh."

Daiki bumped into his shoulder. "Did you expect I'd say fire-engine red?"

"No… yes." Sage laughed.

"Well, it's not. That leans more toward the blue base rather than yellow."

Sage nodded at the art lesson, and the tension he carried begin to drop away.

"Come on. The crowd isn't bad considering the season and the time of day." They caught groups and then passed them. Now with no one near them, they were able to walk up the mountain side by side.

A light breeze blew through the trees as birds chirped while flying from branch to branch. Animals scuttled through the underbrush near the stone steps.

Daiki's fluid movements as he took the stairs were a turn-on. Who would have thought someone could climb stairs in a sexy way, but may the messengers of the gods help Sage, because Daiki did.

And thank the gods his erection issues really had been simply stress. He didn't want to go on ED meds just yet. But hiking up a mountain with an erection wasn't his idea of fun, so he stopped studying Daiki's every move and focused on the forest surrounding them.

He looked around. "I'm not seeing any of the monkeys the signs warn about."

"And we probably won't. Since people stopped feeding them, they stay away from the path for the most part. Oh hey, look. It's late in the season, but being higher up, there are still some cherry blossoms in the distance." Daiki took a picture with his phone, but Sage was positive he'd rather have sketched the trees.

Along the path of the torii gates, low grasses, moss, and lush trees flanked them and shaded their way up.

Sage wanted to confirm what his quick research had shown, so he asked, "From what I googled on the train, therapy isn't popular here, is it?"

"It's rare, and to find a therapist is difficult." Daiki handed one of the water bottles to Sage and took a sip from the other.

Sage sighed and took a long drink. "And I also saw lots of the medications you can get in the States aren't legal here."

"Well, certain ones. But there are some exceptions and there might be some different options." Daiki took the bottle of water back and put them both in his messenger bag.

Not wanting to be an exception, Sage shrugged. But wasn't that the issue Kashi-sei wanted to address? Being different wasn't a problem, it simply *was*. He thought out loud, "Maybe I can look at those options and get some antianxiety meds."

Daiki nodded. "There's some herbal medicines like Agaranzai, which helps lessen anxiety caused by speaking in public. You might want to look into something like that."

"Yeah, thanks." Herbal or chemical or both… Sage was determined to find something that would work.

"We'll find a way for you to do what you want." Daiki appeared confident. Sage absorbed some of that assurance.

Stopping at the lookout, they took some selfies.

Sage posted to his Instagram and Twitter feed. "Got to keep fresh content."

The people hiking up the stairs had thinned out considerably at the lookout point. Either they decided they'd had enough steps and were headed back down, or they stopped at the restaurant.

Sage and Daiki passed the smaller shrines with stone tablets and many with fox statues.

Feeling lucky, Sage found his confidence growing. With Daiki and the band's help, he'd figure this stage fright stuff out.

By the time they got to a row of shops and another restaurant, Sage was relaxed.

"Let's go in here." Daiki pointed out a tea shop with souvenirs and sweets in the window.

"Sure." Sitting down would be nice.

A woman in her late sixties brought over a pot of delicious-smelling green tea and two cups and whispered to Daiki, "He's going to be thrilled to see you."

Daiki poured the tea with total focus, as if it was a complex process, though Sage was sure Daiki was avoiding his gaze.

"Daiki? Who is she—"

"Daiki! Why didn't you tell me you were coming?" An older gentleman leaned a bit on the woman who'd brought their tea as he hurried over to their table.

Daiki stood and bowed, and then the older man pulled him into his arms for a hug. "Grandfather." The warmth with which Daiki said the word told Sage how important the man was to him.

Sage jumped to his feet and tried not to feel self-conscious and nervous.

Why hadn't Daiki toldl him they'd be meeting his grandfather? Sage would have liked to prepare and would have brought a present to give him.

When the hug ended, Daiki introduced Sage.

He'd never felt like a greeting was such a test before, but he was determined to make the best impression he could. Sage preferred to err on the side of formality.

Daiki gave Sage a reassuring smile and then explained, "I didn't tell Sage he'd be meeting you. Partly because I couldn't remember if you'd be up here this weekend or next. And since you refuse to have a cell phone—"

"It's okay. You're here. I'm here. And I've met your friend." That seemed like an ongoing discussion that Daiki's grandfather waved off.

Daiki and Sage retook their seats after the older man sat down.

He squinted and looked between Sage and Daiki. "How long have you loved each other?"

Daiki squeaked, "Grandfather! What do you mean? We've only just met."

His grandfather chuckled and muttered, "I thought I was the one with the bad vision."

"You accept your grandson?" The question fell out of Sage's mouth before he could call the words back.

Daiki's grandfather sipped his tea and smiled. "What's to accept? Reality is what it is. We can fight against our true selves and deny the truth, but it's fruitless. Reality and truth remain as constants. Now I ask again, how long have you loved each other?"

Sage decided to make the most of the opportunity. "Almost from the first day I met him, sir."

Daiki leaned back, and his mouth dropped open.

Daiki's grandfather leaned forward. "Do tell."

Grinning, Sage was happy to share. "We attended a meeting together, and Daiki dropped a teacup. I couldn't stop staring at him. It was like everything got completely quiet. All I could hear was my heart beating for him."

"Good man. Not everyone is willing to listen to what their heart is saying."

Daiki's grandfather must have approved because the rest of the time he plied Sage with special teas and sweets.

After about two hours, Daiki's grandfather insisted they leave before it got too close to dusk.

They said their goodbyes and started the hike down the steps.

Through the trees, Sage could see the fiery colors of the setting sun. "Look at those oranges."

Daiki nodded and pointed out, "Various shades of orange, yes, but see the golds, and on that side, it almost goes to plum."

Charmed yet again, Sage couldn't help but tease. "So orangey purple?"

"Plum," Daiki insisted, like this was a line he'd not cross.

Sage laughed. "Okay, got it. Plum. I bet that look of abject horror is the same I'd wear if you suggested I use no-name drumheads. Come on, we should be down before it's dark."

"I could do these paths blindfolded—wait, that's it." Daiki yanked him to a stop as his words bounced through the trees. Several birds sitting on the torii gates they were under squawked and flew away.

"What?" Sage stared at him, trying to read his mind but failing.

"You don't need to see your drums to play them, right?"

"Of course not." Sage used the same drums configuration he'd perfected in middle school.

Daiki's grin seemed to light the twilight. "How about a blindfold?"

Unable to restrain himself, Sage snarked, "Kinky, but what do you mean?"

Barely sparing him a wink to acknowledge Sage's wildly funny reference, Daiki continued, "One of the things I'm struggling with in Kashi-sei's manga is that everything is too perfect, but wouldn't this be the exact thing you want to share with the audience?"

"That I started a band without realizing I have stage fright?" Sage put all the "are you serious" he could fit into his tone.

"You've got an issue, and you're working through it. You're not ignoring your mental health. There's no shame to this struggle, and it's not meant to be hidden, but highlighted. Isn't Kashi-sei all about visibility?"

Sexy and smart. Sage congratulated himself on falling for Daiki. "Fuck, you're not wrong but—"

"If it's too personal to include, I understand." Daiki began trudging down the stairs again.

"No, you're right. This is my internal struggle, and allowing the fans to see me overcome it or crash and burn is how it should be." Sage should be honest if he needed medicine to allow him on stage. "America has a huge problem with stigma about using legal chemical intervention for enhancing the quality of life, which seems crazy since too many self-medicate with alcohol and nonlegal drugs."

Daiki nodded and then asked, "Do you think hearing the crowd but not seeing actual people might help?"

Sage was afraid to say. "Yeah, maybe. It's worth a try, along with that herbal medicine or something else you mentioned earlier…. What?"

Daiki hugged him tight. "I really think this is going to work."

"And if it doesn't?" Sage couldn't help but worry.

Shrugging, Daiki said, "Then we try something else. If that doesn't work, you know what we do?"

Sage laughed. His heart was light with happiness. "Yeah, we try something else."

He'd never really been part of a *we*. The *we* counterbalanced much of his stress.

It wasn't him alone dealing with his fear, but Daiki as well. And the band and maybe even their fans would be supportive, and in turn his sharing might help some of them.

Mission accomplished.

Chapter 17

As soon as Daiki and Sage returned from Inari and stepped into the apartment, the band lined up to question Sage. The guys wanted to reassure themselves Sage wouldn't be quitting.

"I'll answer all your questions, but first someone needs to fill me in on this whole *Butterscotch* thing." Sage's grin morphed into a resigned smile directed at Daiki.

Ah, the Pause button was now pushed on their covert groping on the train, which had continued in the taxi. Daiki could be patient.

"Well, let me tell you—" Zen's words became muffled by Haru's hand over his mouth as he was dragged into the band room.

"I'll see you in a bit." Sage pulled Daiki into his arms. "Thank you."

Daiki never expected to be hugged so much in his life, but he snuggled Sage back tight and then released him. "Go."

Sage's hand landed on Daiki's butt and he rubbed. "Okay, but later...."

Nodding, Daiki took their bags to the laundry room. He threw a small load in the washer and headed to their bedroom.

Their bedroom... his grandfather approved, as he'd expected him to, but he still was relieved.

And Sage had basically admitted he loved Daiki. They hadn't discussed that new bit, but Daiki felt like his heart was made of pure rainbows.

He grabbed his sketch pad and let his hand and mind loose on the page.

Hard to believe a gorgeous drummer was in love with him. He was definitely writing his own manga. Glancing down at the paper in front of him, he paused. He'd drawn the beginnings of a wedding scene.

Did he want that? He flipped the page on that question because that was best left for another day. First he wanted to make sure Sage was on the right track with overcoming his stage fright. And then, if he were writing his own story....

"Oh," Daiki gasped as the lights in the room flicked on. He glanced at the door to see Sage smiling at him.

Sage said, "I think we should get the lights on a sensor so they turn on when it gets dark."

"I could still see." Daiki grumbled and rubbed his eyes. Then he set aside his sketch pad and stretched. Every bone in his back and neck either popped, cracked, or both.

"I also think we should look into a drafting table and a proper chair like you have in your studio, along with a computer setup." Sage held out sketch pads and a thumb drive.

"That's a good idea." Daiki accepted the items. "What's this?"

"Art from Zen's sister. He said there's no rush and asked if you would be willing to give her honest feedback. He'd appreciate it."

"Of course I will." Daiki set the pads and thumb drive on the shelf. "How did it go with the band?"

"I guess they really aren't letting me replace myself." Sage pulled out the elastic holding back the front of his hair and rubbed his fingers across the top of his head.

Daiki grinned. "I didn't think you'd be able to convince them."

"Mm, yeah. I didn't try too hard. So tomorrow I want to get that herbal med you mentioned. Zen already booked another gig. He says this venue is smaller, but his definition of small and mine I'm pretty sure are different."

Daiki nodded. "When?"

"Next Friday." Sage twisted his hands in front of him.

"That's only a bit more than a week away."

"I know. He has also scheduled us at increasingly larger venues over the next three months." Sage sounded anxious and annoyed in equal parts. "I didn't think Zen would be able to move so quickly. Though Haru said it's a way to help desensitize me."

"Also, it's a more natural progression for musicians to start smaller, then work their way up. You jumped from no audience to big with no buildup." Daiki could see the panels of the manga in his head unfolding. The growing crowd size with each page turned. His man sitting behind the drums, looking incredibly sexy in a blindfold. Shirt draped off one shoulder....

"What are you thinking?" Sage asked as if he could see how delicious and explicit Daiki's mental storyboards had started to turn.

"Me kneeling behind the bass drum during a show, sucking—"

"Is it later?" Sage stared at him.

"Hm, it is," Daiki said.

Sage grabbed him out of the chair.

Whoosh, the air rushed out of him as his back hit the wall, but his heart beat faster. "Sage?"

Sage's other hand slapped the wall on the other side of Daiki's head. "Yes, Daiki?"

Daiki tried to inhale, but the air got stuck. He attempted to look down, but Sage lowered his head so they maintained eye contact.

"Let's finish what you started on the train." Sage opened both of their jeans. His lips trailed along Daiki's jaw, sending shivers of want through him.

"I didn't start anything... much." Daiki should help, but he stayed pressed against the wall. He surrendered to the achy and needy feelings that erupted whenever Sage touched him.

"You didn't, huh?" Sage smirked and then nuzzled his neck. He pushed Daiki's pants out of the way.

"Oh God," Daiki moaned as Sage wrapped a hand around both of their shafts.

Sage glanced down, as did Daiki.

Their erections pressed together, providing an unfamiliar but delicious heated friction.

Usually Daiki didn't get hard this fast, but they were both erect and leaking. The hours between the train and now vanished.

He wanted this never to end. The desire to stay suspended in pleasure had gone to his head.

Sage's gaze burned him on the way to his eyes. "You wanna come?"

The direct words shocked and excited Daiki in equal measure, making denial impossible. He thrust his shaft into Sage's fist, trying to rush toward orgasm.

Loosening his grip, Sage asked, "Do you?"

Daiki's breath caught. To admit such a thing… he'd never. But if Sage demanded his confession, he'd comply. "Yes, Sage. Make me come. I want to come, please. Please, Sage."

"Fuck, your begging—it does something to me. Pleading with me heals something in me. Seeing you always controlled and measured until I get my hands on you, around you, and then—"

Is that why Sage needed his admission? He'd gladly give it. "I'm your slutty uke wanting nothing more than to come for you again and again. I'd do anything for you, Sage. Anything. Please…. Oh, coming—" The last part morphed into a shuddering groan.

"Yes." Sage gasped. His head dropped onto Daiki's shoulder, and within a few strokes he came too.

They cleaned up and slid into bed.

Sage pulled Daiki onto his shoulder and then tucked the blanket around them. "You still haven't asked me about what I told your grandfather."

Daiki was tempted to play clueless but couldn't. "Did you want me to?"

Chuckling, Sage nodded.

He'd never shared his feelings before, not that he had many to share. One glance at Sage told him he wanted to try.

Daiki took a deep breath and exhaled. "I love you. It's not because I've been drawing someone who looks like you, but I like spending time with you. You make me smile. Your dares make me step past my usual boundaries. I adore that you're traditional but a bit unpredictable. I want to spend a very long time with you, crossing things off our list and adding more so we're never done with it or each other."

Daiki pressed his lips together, not sure if that could stop the emotions swirling in him but hoping the words would stop flooding out.

Sage hugged him tight. "Thank you. At the risk of being everything you expect an emotional American to be, I love you too. You are everything I didn't know I wanted. I don't have to settle for less than what I need with you. Maybe I'm crazy for admitting this so soon, but I want us to be together as a long-term thing, whatever happens with the band."

Inhaling sharply, Daiki sat up so he could see Sage's face.

Sincerity and affection painted Sage in the glorious colors of love, and he said, "You're the life partner I want by my side always… and forever."

Rainbows of happiness sparked around him.

Daiki wouldn't have believed he could love Sage any more than he had a moment ago, but the man's words proved him wrong in the best possible way. His heart expanded with more love and affection.

Words wouldn't come out, so he simply rolled into Sage and hugged him tight.

THE NEXT morning, Daiki woke squinting at the not completely closed curtains. He shivered. Sage had stolen the covers again. He'd have to get another throw to defend against the thief he slept with.

After pushing himself out of bed, Daiki took care of life in the bathroom.

As he walked back into the room, his breath caught. What was a beautiful bleached-blond drummer, with his lips still swollen from last night, doing in his bed? Catching sight of the love bruises Sage wore on his neck and left shoulder reminded Daiki this was not a storyboard. This was real life. *His* real life.

Not sure how he got here but glad to have finally made it to happy, Daiki wanted Sage to steal all the covers for his entire life.

A soft ping notified him he had an email, probably from Akihiro.

Though his feedback would probably yank Daiki from the land of happy, he opened the message anyway.

Wow, for Akihiro this was glowing feedback. His pages and the changes in the story worked!

Moving in with Sage hadn't affected his art negatively. If anything, Daiki might be more productive.

Sage snuffled in his sleep and then put the covers over his head.

Daiki grabbed the work from Zen's sister. Flipping the cover of the first sketch pad over, he eased into the chair.

Yumi's style captured his attention with its sharpness and directness. Good strong lines cut across the pages, telling the story with crystal-clear accuracy. Yumi appeared reluctant to utilize shadow and black spaces, but each panel moved the stories along, though possibly a bit too fast. Although Yumi needed to find patience and let the stories unfold at a slower pace, overall, he was impressed.

Daiki plugged the thumb drive into his laptop and saw more of the same. Zen's sister was talented. He retrieved the card and then sent an email with his feedback, suggestions, and an offer to look over her—or perhaps it would be their—portfolio for art school when the time came.

Sage stretched and reached over to Daiki's side of the bed. Whining when he found it empty, he kept touching the bed as if to make Daiki appear.

Setting aside his computer, Daiki slid back into bed.

The conscious Sage covered Daiki with blankets and snuggled into him. "Morning."

"Good morning. We should get up." Though he didn't know why.

Sage thrust against Daiki's thigh and snorted. "I already am."

He dragged Daiki out of bed and into the bathroom for an interesting and satisfying shower, which made them decide going back to bed was the best decision ever.

Even though Sage was still stressed, it appeared not to be affecting everything anymore.

Eventually, as they decided to get dressed, Sage said, "I should make a vlog."

Daiki began to gather his things. "Okay, I'll go in the other room."

Sage nabbed his hand like Daiki had suggested he go on a walkabout. "You can stay."

Daiki couldn't say no to the big eyes Sage used as a weapon to take away his will. "Sure. I'll be over here drawing."

After a few minutes, Sage stopped pacing and sat in front of his computer. "Hey, voiders. It's Sage Nakamura. Welcome to *Scream Into the Void*. Are you ready to hear me holler?"

Daiki tried not to stare, but Sage was quite impressive. His free hair cascaded around his face; Daiki needed to capture that bounce on the page. Sage's vlogging voice dropped deeper than usual, and his vlog was in English. Hearing Sage's deep voice speaking foreign words made Daiki go a bit uke.

Sage's voice washed over Daiki, making him want. What would Sage do if Daiki slipped under...?

"Many of you have asked for an update on my band, Kashi-sei. So here it is." Pointing like there was something in front of him Sage said, "Like, subscribe, comment, but don't offer me sexual favors. I'm taken."

Sexual favors? Daiki would be happy to, but Sage mesmerized him.

Sage caught Daiki gawking and gave him a crooked smile that could ignite all the paper in his sketch pad. Then he turned back to the camera. "'Cause now I'm part of a *we*, so you horny bitches can stop sending the dick pic links and dirty suggestions in the comment section. Anyway, you know the routine.

"Back to the update. Here's a fun fact. Did you know you might have stage fright and not even realize it?" Wow, right out of the gate. Sage really was fearless. "I found this out at a very convenient time… minutes before Kashi-sei's debut show."

With too much cuteness, Sage cupped his ear. "What's that, you ask? How could I be such a dope not to know a huge crowd would freak me out? Great question…. Ah, what's that? How did I deal with the situation?"

Sage shrugged as he exhaled hard. He set aside the cue cards he shuffled. "I guess this little confessional isn't as easy as my index cards led me to believe. What-the-fuck-ever. I'm going to keep giving you the truth whether you want it or not. Yeah, I'm an idiot, so there's that. But skipping to how did I deal with my stage fright? I didn't. I fled the scene like a murderer. I shit you not. I come to Japan to start a band, find talented musicians, and then I flee prior to our first show."

Shaking his head, he sighed. "Here on my YouTube channel, as much as some of you don't think I edit, I do. I also reshoot, delete, and add. But as I stepped onto that stage, I realized there were no redos. Anxiety is a horrific task master."

That was truth. Reality didn't come with an eraser.

"This is it. You screw up, you can't go edit that out. Your mistake will live forever. I left the stage and my band to do what any other unstable LAer would do. I got rip-roaring drunk. Bad move? You bet. Fortunately, there were people who had my back. Like my boyfriend.

"Now the next part, I know several of you will think I orchestrated it, but my boyfriend took me to the Inari shrine to work out my issues. I swear. I climbed a mountain of torii gates and got answers—well, possible answers. I say possible because I don't know if these will work or if I'll have to find other things. But luckily for me, my band wouldn't let me quit. Yes, I did try. I'm going to use several things to survive getting on that stage."

Smiling, Sage glanced off camera at Daiki again. "The reason why I'm no longer accepting generous sexual offers reminded me that's what

Kashi-sei is about. Yeah, my boyfriend is much smarter than me. He pointed out being visible is about being yourself and loving yourself even with flaws and mistakes."

Daiki didn't deserve so much credit. He shook his head.

Sage nodded and mouthed, "Thank you."

Turning back to the camera, Sage continued, "My good friend Ryder has always said visibility is showing exactly who you are. Sharing things you don't even want to look at yourself, and fuck it. They're right. There might be someone out there watching this or the band who will get something valuable from me sharing this bit of my humanity… one of my many imperfections, if you will."

Sage took a sip of his probably now cold green tea. "So how am I going to accomplish getting my ass on stage and staying there? I really don't know, but there's an herbal remedy along with, get this… a blindfold. Yup, I'm going to go onstage in a blindfold."

Waving a strip of fabric around, Sage grinned and then set it aside. He held up the picture he'd asked Daiki to draw yesterday. The colorful drawing showed Sage shirtless behind the drums, wearing a black blindfold. Getting a good look at the sketch, he grinned. "I look sexy, right?"

Daiki stopped himself from nodding. Penning those drumming muscles of Sage's had aroused him deeply, which evolved into a glorious time.

"Well, more on that in the upcoming manga. The links to the artist and a preorder for the manga are right here." Sage pointed to nothing again.

After a bit more on the band, Sage signed off.

"How was that?" The uncertainty bled out in Sage's tone.

"Great." Daiki smiled and turned his pad around. He'd drawn Sage dancing down the steps of the Inari shrine in a blindfold. "And yes, you look very sexy!"

Sage strutted around the room with a smug smirk. He arched his eyebrow and lifted his chin. "Really?"

"Yeah, really, and since there are no redos in life, I think we should go back to bed so I can convince you that you are as sexy as I draw you."

Grinning, Sage was already pulling down the covers.

Chapter 18

SAGE ENDED the song with a six-stroke roll on the drums. The pure sound bounced off their practice room walls and seeped into his bones.

Haru nodded his approval. "Good add."

Rehearsal had been going well for days. Now if Sage could just translate that into confidence, maybe he'd feel ready for the show tomorrow night.

Without a doubt, he loved working with the band. If he was forced to choose between playing with the band or alone, he would, surprisingly, pick the band. The immediate feedback from someone not behind glass, staring at the sound board, was beyond reinforcing, and the synergy the group created fed his soul.

The doorbell rang.

"I'll get it." Zen hustled out of the music room.

Within a minute, Zen strolled back in.

"Who was it?" Wayuu asked.

Zen shrugged. "Just some people."

"Some people?" Sage asked.

"A few people who are running our fan club?"

What? Since when did Kashi-sei have a fan club?

"Fan club? Nice." Haru gave a happy guitar riff.

Sage wanted to ask how many there were, but he settled for "Where are they?"

"In the other room. Why?" Zen squinted at him and made a "you're losing it, bro" face.

Nervousness that people would hear them practice tried to skitter through him, but it was probably only two or three people. Sage pointed out the obvious, "Shouldn't we go talk to them?"

"Nah, they said they'd enjoy some tea until we're done. We've got two more songs in this set, don't we?" Zen asked like he didn't remember.

Without rolling his eyes, which took an impressive amount of effort, Sage said, "Fine. If you don't think it's rude—"

"I take people at their word." Zen smiled at him, and then his gaze slid over to Wayuu.

Wayuu immediately glued his stare onto Sage. "Ready?"

What the…? As long as whatever Wayuu and Zen had going on didn't affect the music, Sage would keep his mouth shut. He gave a nod and then tapped his sticks together. "Five, six, seven, eight."

The song slid into another seamlessly.

Sage ended the fast beat by slamming to a hard stop.

Applause flooded the room.

Sage glanced at the door to find half a dozen people clapping and smiling. Shock smashed into him at the number of people who'd heard him play live. Was that Zen's plan?

"Zen?"

Zen twirled over to him as if he wasn't a scheming mastermind. "We'll chat later about how you survived your first live performance. Right now, we should talk to our fan club."

A gush of excited squeals sounded as Haru, Wayuu, and Zen were swallowed up by the small crowd.

Maybe Sage should be mad, but Zen had warned him he planned on helping Sage get desensitized to an audience any way he could.

He had played knowing there were people listening, but he didn't want to get carried away. After all, not too many people could fit in their apartment.

Sage set his sticks down and joined his bandmates, who were mingling with not a dozen, but close to twenty people.

Two guys and a girl stepped over to him. The taller guy said, "Man, you guys are so talented. The show is going to be fantastic."

"Thank you. My bandmates are great."

"Don't be modest." The other guy did an air drum solo ending with a flourish. "I cannot wait until tomorrow night."

"I watch your YouTube channel. I love your videos," said the young woman in English.

Many of the people came over and expressed similar positive affirmations. Every one of them promised to be at the show cheering for him.

"Maybe this won't be so bad," Sage whispered to Haru.

THE HOUSE lights were on, which allowed Sage a clear view of all the chairs and tables. So many! Anxiety tackled him. He wiped his forehead and turned back to the band. "It's bad. It's really bad."

"Take the medicine. You've had no side effects when you tried it, so let's see if it helps," Daiki suggested for the third time.

Right, the medicine would calm him.

He was having trouble catching his breath, so his thoughts weren't quite coherent over the buzz in his brain. "Daiki, I—"

Haru glared at him. "I thought Americans were all about therapy and enhanced living through herbal and chemical intervention. Or do you think people who need medication to control an issue are weak?"

"It's not that. Just…." Sage struggled to find the words. "It's hard to reach for help."

"No reaching necessary. Open." Daiki was there, and he dropped the tablet into Sage's mouth and handed him water.

He swallowed the damned little pill, and even that action made Sage feel he was more in control. Maybe he could do this.

Wayuu shook his head and did some stretches. "You got this, Sage."

Sage opened his mouth, but Daiki stepped behind him. "You'll probably start feeling a bit calmer by the end of your sound check."

"Just having you next to me is doing that." This time around, while anxiety was riding him, having people in his corner, especially Daiki, made him more willing to believe he had a hope of overriding the pressure.

Haru called out, "Sound check."

Zen hurried after him. "Right behind you, Butterscotch."

Ichika folded her arms over her chest, stepped in front of Zen, and glared. "We discussed this."

Shaking his head, Zen claimed, "I'm only teasing."

"I'm the only one who may call him that." Her sharp words weren't dulled by the sweet smile she gave him.

Sage had learned great respect for Ichika. She was all cuddly bunny with Haru and killer rabbit with anyone who messed with him.

Growling, Haru glared at Zen as he strapped on his bass.

Sage moved behind the drums, and the sound check went without a hitch.

AFTER TOO short a time, Wayuu stopped jumping and announced, "It's showtime."

Already?

Sage swallowed hard and peered into the bar. Every seat was filled, and people lined the walls. The room grew. Too big.

"Hey, only a little bit more than you already played for… right?" Zen's concerned smile didn't reach his eyes.

"Not helping." Sage backed around behind the boxes that doubled as a privacy wall. He focused on his breathing. His chest hurt, and it was hot.

Daiki rubbed his shoulders. "Think past the show to later…."

"Later?" Sage tried to put a purr in his voice.

Daiki had promised in great detail that whatever happened on stage wouldn't affect their private aftershow party.

"Yes, later." Daiki smirked at him and stepped in front of him. With all the boldness of one of his characters, Daiki grazed his hand over Sage's erection.

Right here… behind some boxes. They weren't even behind a curtain!

Sage tried to say something, but his words came out as grumbled desperation. Another first with Daiki.

Daiki gave him a hungry look.

"Daiki, I—"

Zen grabbed Sage's wrists as if suspicious he would flee. Okay, probably a good precaution, with his record. "Hey, Daiki. You've got the blindfold?"

Daiki pulled a strip of black fabric from his pocket.

As Sage leaned in, he inhaled the leather jacket Daiki wore, along with everything he was.

"Keep me in your head. You're playing for just me." Daiki secured the fabric around Sage's eyes and then gave him a deep, toe-curling kiss.

Display of affection in public?

Wishing he could see Daiki's cheeks tint, Sage muttered in English, "Well, damn. Fuck me."

"Whenever you want. All you've got to do is ask," Daiki reminded him, as if he didn't recall the offer.

Images of Daiki taking him flashed through his mind. "Oh, um—"

"I wonder if you'll ask me tonight… or if we won't make it out of the club. You haven't been blown in a club bathroom in far too long." Daiki sounded like he was reading from one of his mangas. Maybe he was, but wow, that was a book Sage wanted to read.

Daiki swiped a wet finger over Sage's lower lip.

Lust barreled into Sage. "You're trying to kill me."

"No, simply reminding you of priorities." Daiki hugged him, which allowed them to be pressed together.

Sage shivered. He turned his head and dragged his lips against Daiki's neck.

Zen cleared his throat. "Sage, just 'cause you can't see us doesn't mean we can't see you."

Haru chuckled.

"But hey, way to solve stage fright." Zen snorted right next to Sage and then shoulder-bumped him.

"Do you want Daiki to walk you out, or one of us?" Wayuu asked in his serious band-related voice.

"Daiki." Sage wanted the excuse to wrap an arm around him.

Daiki guided him around the boxes and onto the darkened stage to his seat behind the drums. He kept sliding his hand over Sage's ass.

"You going to put this in the manga too?" If Sage could think past his interest in later, he might be curious.

The chuckle Daiki gave him was dark and lit him on fire. "I'm going to put something somewhere."

An "Oh" escaped Sage because he didn't see the slap on the side of his ass coming when Daiki's hand connected to his butt.

Daiki rested his hands on Sage's thighs and leaned in. "Later. Whatever happens out here won't change…. See you in a bit."

Dirty flashes of the promised later taunted Sage. Sexual frustration wasn't pleasant, but it sure beat brain-eating anxiety. The medicine must have kicked in, or maybe it was his focus on *later*….

A bit of laughter, the clinking of glasses, scraping of chairs, coughs, and snippets of conservation drifted from the audience. They were there, but not seeing them helped.

"Count us in," Zen demanded from somewhere in front of Sage.

"One, two, three." He tapped his sticks and then depended on muscle memory and the song to guide his hands.

He cautiously opened his eyes behind the blindfold. The strip of fabric made seeing hard, but not impossible. He decided to close his eyes again—not out of fear but wanting to feel the connection with the music and his band.

At the end of the first song, a million-year pause ensued between Haru's last note on his bass and the crowd erupting in applause.

After drinking in the love, Zen greeted the crowd. "We welcome you to the first real debut of all the members of Kashi-sei. The English word is *visibility*, and that's what we want to accomplish. We want to make great music and allow fans to be themselves. Kashi-sei will lead by example. We will try to be our authentic selves, though between you and me, that might not look as expected. We hope not to disappoint, but Kashi-sei will be a band that celebrates the different and the uniqueness in all of us. Thank you for your open minds."

The audience applauded. Though in truth they would have clapped if Zen talked utter nonsense, because he was Suzuki Zen.

He introduced himself and then Wayuu. As if the two idols wouldn't be recognized. Then he handed the audience over to Wayuu.

"In terms of being more me...." Wayuu must have taken off his leather jacket to reveal his sparkly purple T-shirt with a unicorn in bondage on it, if the gasps, then applause, were anything to go by. "Allow me to introduce Yamamoto Haru-san. He just needs to hear something once before it's his."

Haru gave a small riff of agreement on his strings.

Wayuu continued, "The man behind the drums is also the man behind Kashi-sei's concept. He brought us all together."

The crowd clapped and chanted his name. "Sage! Sage! Sage!"

Holy fuck! That didn't happen in the studio. He felt pleased, humbled, and psyched all at the same time and waved his drumsticks.

"Oh, yeah, about the blindfold. Sage is either shy or kinky." Wayuu's playfulness did have a way of making everything sexual.

"Can't he be both?" Zen asked, much to the audience's elation.

Sage gave a rim shot.

"Most definitely. I hope he is," Wayuu purred and then continued, "In light of that possibility, here's our next song. You might have seen pics floating around, or if you were really lucky, a naughty little clip."

Way to own it, Way!

Counting the band in felt good. Playing was awesome. Performing in front of an audience... well, the jury was still out. But he survived.

When Sage stepped back around the boxes after their last encore, he sagged in relief and took off his blindfold.

He'd done it.

Daiki gave him a hungry look as he showed him a sign in scroll letters that read "Bathroom out of order. Please use other one."

Sage couldn't think of a better way to celebrate surviving.

The same could not be said for the soap dispenser in the bathroom. He or Daiki or maybe both of them backed into the container and slammed it off the wall. Luckily it had been out of soap for a while.

Daiki looked shocked when Sage dropped to his knees. "What are you doing?"

Why? "Didn't you say it had been a while since you've been blown in a bathroom?"

"No, I said—" Whatever Daiki meant to say was lost to his moans.

Sage sucked harder.

TIME'S BEAT kept ticking on, and the summer concert season was here.

Sage glanced around. This was by far the biggest place the band had played. The venues had steadily grown in size, but this was much larger than their original debut, when he'd bolted.

He poked his head back around the curtain to look out. There were at least twice as many people packed in as had attended the concert he'd ghosted. He shook his head—as if that would help him figure out what to do.

"You did fine in sound check," Haru reminded him.

"Yeah, but now there's people." Sage frowned and pointed at the closed curtain.

Zen arched his eyebrow. "That tends to happen, especially when you sell tickets."

Haru snapped his fingers. "That's where we went wrong."

Even as his heart began to race, Sage couldn't help laughing. "Shut up, both of you."

Ichika cleared her throat from the corner.

"Oops. Sorry, Ichika. I was joking."

Her frown became a smile. "I know, Sage. I'm teasing."

Zen stomped his foot. "That's not fair! Why does Sage get to—"

She narrowed her eyes on Zen and then arched her eyebrow at him as if she was daring him to continue whining.

Holding his hands out in front of him, Zen shook his head. "Fine."

"Are you pouting?" Sage teased as he tried to hold it together.

"Of course not. But let's admit she's not being fair." Zen sniffed.

Teasing aside, reality seeped in, making Sage swallow hard. "There's a lot of people out there."

Wayuu was doing his preshow jumping. He bounced over. "This feeling you have—"

"You mean terror?" Sage wanted to be clear.

"Yes, that. It's actually excitement."

"Excitement?" Sage could feel the medicine trying to calm his ass down, but his anxiety still kept him wanting to scale the walls. He took the second pill, which was the limit.

"Doesn't matter how big or small the place we play in, you're the drummer. Everything goes at your pace." Zen gathered them in a huddle. "Besides, we are awesome. When we go out on that stage, whatever happens, happens."

"That's what I'm worried about." Sage pointed out the obvious, which seemed to be lost on these three.

Wayuu and Zen stood on either side of Sage. They were in the idol zone, so nothing seemed to touch them. Even Haru seemed fascinated by the glitter and glam flowing from their aura.

Zen glanced at Wayuu for a moment and then gave Sage a small smile. He seemed to understand what they were exuding. "You want to feel this… be this?"

Who wouldn't? Sage nodded.

"Take it. No one is going to give you this feeling, not even the fans. You've got to know in your heart that this is what you were born to do," Zen challenged him.

Wayuu looked him dead in the eyes with all his idol power and said, "This is your dream. Live it."

Haru pointed at Wayuu and Zen. "Yes! This is what I'm talking about. I'm pumped. Sage?"

Sage gave a halfhearted nod.

Zen gripped him tighter into the circle. "Have no doubt. We will screw up. Haru will miss a chord. You'll come in slow, or I'll miss a note. It doesn't matter. Own. All of it. It's part of us. This isn't about being perfect. This is about showing the world who we are. Letting people know they can show who they are. If you were serious about making a difference, this is what we've been working for. You learn more from your mistakes than getting it right."

"Yes." Sage nodded. He'd accept all the crazy shit that might happen and then embrace the imperfections. Their goal wasn't to be perfect but to make mistakes and keep on going. If he wasn't strong enough to do it, how could he encourage their fans to be who they were?

"We've got each other's back. Kashi-sei on three." Zen counted for them.

"Kashi-sei!"

Where was Daiki? Sage turned.

Daiki was there behind him. He blindfolded Sage and guided him onto the stage. Sage had taken the herbal a bit earlier, so it was kicking in right on time.

"No wicked promises?" Sage found he didn't need the distraction but wanted something to look forward to.

"No promises, just a question. Can I be inside you after the show?"

Sage tried to form a sentence, but since he couldn't even get a word past his lips, he gave a nod. When Daiki hadn't followed up on his original suggestion, he'd figured Daiki wasn't into it... but apparently he'd been wrong.

"I can't wait," Daiki said in Sage's ear as one of his hands traced over Sage's ass.

Sage swallowed hard and tried to process everything.

The crowd began chanting "Kashi-sei."

Daiki was going to top him. It had been a while, so—

He opened his eyes. The light peeked through the blindfold. Though it might be a train coming at him. "Fuck, I might as well enjoy the ride."

"Later, I'll give you whatever kind of ride you'd like." Daiki's breath caressed the side of Sage's face, and then he disappeared.

The stage lights came on, and the crowd went crazy.

Sage was in his spot behind his drums, and he adjusted his blindfold. The fabric was stretched a little thin, so he could see the shadows of his bandmates.

Wayuu and Zen looked over their shoulders at him. Lights found and outlined Haru, who raised his chin to Sage.

"Five, six, seven, eight," he counted them in.

The first three songs went as planned, but then Wayuu's mic cut out. Sage had a moment of panic. *What the hell were they going to do?*

Wayuu shrugged and danced in place.

Zen strutted over with his mic, and they sang the song together, their voices harmonizing. The notes were brighter, and the lyrics had even more emotion weaved into them.

The thirsty crowd went even crazier.

Zen told the crowd, "Sometimes things go wrong. Like hell-in-a-handbasket wrong—"

Wayuu stuck his mouth near the mic. "Hell in a what?"

"Kashi-sei is about screwing up and being okay with that." Zen sounded like he was grinning.

"We're about being different and celebrating it," Wayuu added.

Sage was learning that as well.

Chapter 19

"ARE YOU sure you want to come back here?" Daiki and Sage stood in front of the love hotel they had visited.

"There's a symmetry about being back for another first. Don't you think?" Sage grinned at him.

Daiki swallowed hard. Why was he nervous? They'd had all sorts of sex, in a variety of places. This should be no—

What if he were a terrible top? Or if he couldn't get hard?

"Unless you don't want to. We definitely don't have to do this. So many other things to do." Sage was considerate to a fault.

Daiki wanted to do this, and he'd promised, so he braced himself. "No, I want to try this… if you want to."

Sage slipped his hand into Daiki's and squeezed. "I really do. It's been a while, but I enjoy being penetrated."

Oh. When his Americanness showed, his openness, Sage still had the ability to shock the thoughts out of Daiki.

Once they'd checked in and gathered the treats Sage insisted on, they went to their room.

Setting down the tray, Sage said, "I'll be right back." He went into the bathroom and shut the door.

Daiki stowed two condoms and lubricant under the pillow on the left side. As was their practice during any couple time, he turned off both of their cell phones.

What is taking so long?

He paced around the big, very purple, ruffled bed and then rechecked the supplies. Still there.

Should he undress? Maybe just down to his underwear. He smiled as he put his jeans and T-shirt on the chair. Adjusted the fancy silk underwear Sage had gotten him. They were ultracomfortable and somehow cupped him in a way that made him look more well-endowed than he actually was.

The room had no windows or clocks, and now that the phones were off, Daiki had no idea what time it was. Sage had disappeared into the bathroom about twenty years ago… or maybe it was minutes.

The door opened. Sage emerged in a white robe. The eyeliner he wore for the show hadn't washed off completely, or maybe he'd reapplied it.

Daiki's fingers itched to capture Sage as a picture.

"Hi." Standing in front of Daiki, Sage smiled at him and then looked away.

Daiki's "Hi" came out a little strangled.

Sage kissed him on the cheek. Love painted over the sweet affection of that gesture.

Everything came into focus. Daiki had been drawing sex for over a decade, but tonight he didn't want the filter of art between him and the world. He wanted his life to depict love without the intervention of a storyboard.

Daiki would do his best to show Sage how much he cared with his body and his words.

He took Sage's hands in his own and confessed, "I want to do all my firsts with you, and all my lasts too."

"Oh, Daiki." Sage sounded like he agreed to the unspoken proposal of a lifetime of firsts and lasts.

"What?" Daiki wanted clarity.

"You've been so many of my firsts. You're the first man I've ever loved… and I want you to be my last." Sage closed his eyes and kissed Daiki's hands.

Daiki's breath caught, and only a strangled sound emerged.

Sage chuckled and shook his head. "Maybe that sounds like dialogue from a manga…. But I mean it."

"I couldn't have written it better myself. I love you, and I want to show you how much." Daiki guided him to the bed and laid him out gently.

He hesitated only a moment to capture the image with his heart and then followed him onto the bed.

Sage's robe gaped open a little.

Daiki rested a palm on the warm skin of Sage's chest. He looked serene and calm, but his heart pumped hard and fast.

Skimming a hand down Sage's body, Daiki parted the robe that separated him from Sage. The unfamiliar bath products Sage had used covered his usual scent, but they smelled clean and reminded Daiki of the last time they were here, when Sage took him with such mastery. Daiki doubted he'd have the same skill.

The robe revealed Sage's erection.

Daiki traced a finger around the crown.

"Oh." Sage sighed and thrust.

Maybe skill didn't matter. This was about love, and he certainly could show Sage how he felt by treasuring him.

He stopped staring at the lovely appendage and returned his gaze to meet Sage's.

Sage studied Daiki as if he were judging what he should do. "I prepped myself for you, so I'm good to go when you are."

Daiki wasn't exactly disappointed—not really—but he would have taken care of Sage in that way. "Oh, I thought I could—"

"Next time. I'm just kind of amped up." Sage shifted and pushed against Daiki's fingers.

Daiki removed his hand from Sage's erection and bit back the grin at Sage's whine. "How do you want to lie?"

Sage slipped out of the robe and rolled away from Daiki, presenting him with a lovely view. He glanced over his shoulder. "Could we try it on my side?"

"Of course." Daiki helped him arrange pillows so that Sage would be comfortable and got behind him.

Daiki reached under the pillow and got the supplies. He opened the condom package only to have the rubber spring out and bounce off Sage's back.

Sage half turned. "Can I help?"

"No, I've got it." Trying not to be embarrassed, he shoved off his underwear and kicked it to the floor. Putting a drop of lube in the condom made him feel like this wasn't the first time he was doing this… with another person. Research was one thing, but Daiki's focus shouldn't be on his inexperience, which prevented *perfection*, but on how loving he could make this experience for Sage.

He rolled on the rubber.

Daiki couldn't wait any longer; he coated two fingers and slid them inside of Sage. He caressed them in and out of that warm tightness with a gentle glide.

"Mm, yeah." Sage gripped the pillow in front of him and thrust back, allowing Daiki all the access he could hope for.

"Daiki." His name left Sage's mouth as a moan.

Pulling his fingers out, Daiki coated the already lubed condom with the slippery gel. His strokes helped him regain his full hardness. He set the recapped bottle aside and then traced the crevice of Sage's ass with his covered erection.

Sage leaned his head back against Daiki's shoulder and begged in a soft voice, "Please?"

With all the gentleness he could manage, Daiki slid into Sage a few centimeters. His mind screamed with joy at being inside Sage.

"Yeah, that's good." Sage sighed.

Daiki grabbed the lubricant and added another drop to his erection because the idea of hurting Sage was unthinkable. He evened out the slick and pressed forward with care.

"More, Daiki." Sage wiggled in front of him.

Holding Sage's hip still, Daiki slid slowly and steadily into the tightness until he was as deep as he could go.

"Ah," Sage moaned, like Daiki had given him something he'd been missing his entire life. He tipped his head back with closed eyes and kissed Daiki's jaw. "Rock a bit."

Daiki did. Sensation slammed into him, but it was watching Sage that almost did him in.

"Yeah, more." Sage's eyes remained closed, and he started pushing against Daiki.

A rhythm started. Daiki rolled his hips, inching out.

Sage moaned at the loss and pushed against him harder. With no hesitation Sage was taking what he wanted, and what he wanted was Daiki inside him.

In and out. Daiki tried to focus as he moved.

He wrapped his arms around Sage tighter, holding him close.

The friction increased. Sage kept thrusting back against Daiki.

Sage panted as he said, "Give me your hand."

What? Oh. Daiki wrapped a hand around Sage's erection and stroked.

"Are you going to come?" Sage asked in a worried voice.

Daiki bit his lip. He tried to keep his attention on Sage, but that was what kept nudging him toward the edge. "Soon."

"Not yet," Sage demanded and picked up the pace as he thrust back onto Daiki. "Almost there."

Daiki would try, but oh.... He squeezed his eyes shut.

Sage's loose hair grazed Daiki's shoulder. He thrust his perfect butt, encompassing Daiki in enticing heat.

Riding the edge of sanity, Daiki held on and tried not to fall.

Sage adjusted his angle as he shoved against Daiki. "Ah, yeah... that's it. Right there. Yes—coming!"

Daiki kept thrusting into the impossible tightness, and the heat pulsed all around him. His fist was coated with Sage's orgasm as his body was milked.

Pleasure built in Daiki.

Sage's hand wrapped over his slowed Daiki's strokes, and Sage squeezed Daiki as he continued driving against him. "Come."

Lightning bolted through Daiki as he filled the condom. Orgasm consumed him, but he held on to Sage and eventually found stable ground.

Sage's chuckling roused him.

He stopped pressing kisses on Sage's face and asked, "What?"

"Another first."

Not that it mattered, but Daiki was sure Sage had been with other men in this way—he'd said as much. "I don't understand."

"First time I came while bottoming." Sage turned his head to give him a smirk.

Shock and something that might be pride flooded Daiki, making him need to clarify. "Really?"

"Yup." Sage snorted. "I didn't think I could do that."

A MONTH later, Daiki sat on the balcony and smiled as he read the email from his editor.

Congratulations on your first band series becoming an instant hit. The numbers suggest this is more than

*name recognition. Your fans have welcomed this new
manga starring Kashi-sei, and you've gained readers.*

According to the emails and letters the publisher received, there was a sense of relief and gratefulness. His own fan mail confirmed the sentiment.

The reviews said the Kashi-sei manga, called *See Me*, resonated with all ages. Some were LGBTQ+, others suffered from anxiety, some were fans of the music, and many just wanted to find a community where differences were celebrated. This was better than Daiki had hoped for when he met with his editor all those months ago.

This opportunity not only allowed him to help others find acceptance and an understanding of themselves, but he now accepted who he was. He wrote his own storyboards. Of course, he still had flaws, but he'd found a certain contentment with those parts of himself.

The band had given their approval on the next few story ideas, so it was time to begin some rough storyboards. Needing to think, Daiki slipped out of the apartment and took the elevator to the roof. He meandered through the manicured rooftop garden and over to the glass-enclosed edge. This apartment's roof was much fancier than the one above his studio and with a much better view.

How many times over the years had he stood at a railing and wished for his life to be different?

Tonight, as a gentle breeze blew, he only wanted more of what he had now. His life was exactly where he hoped it would be. His work was finally doing what he desired. And his love life—

"Why are you up here all alone?" Sage's arms wrapped around him, making him feel nearly perfect.

"Just watching the sunset. I didn't want to pull you away from the band." This was better than working on a storyboard… this was working on his life.

Sage hugged him tighter. "I like watching sunsets with you."

Daiki savored this moment of calm. "Me too. Though I need to spend an hour or so drawing tonight."

"No worries. I'm glad the drafting table is working out. I don't want your work to suffer." Sage didn't seem to believe Daiki could work from anywhere, and did. Drawing was air to him; in order to survive he needed to put pen to paper.

"I appreciate that, but it's going well. My assistants have really picked up any slack me working on Kashi-sei has created, which is helping to develop their skills. And actually earlier today I got a couple of emails from my editors. Both publishers have approved several of my unreleased mangas for publication." He'd had fun updating them before submitting them.

Sage chuckled. "I bet they were happy."

"A little too much, but it gives me even more breathing room." Right now he wanted everyone happy. How different his world had become... and how much happier he had become.

"Why do I think you're already working on secret manga besides the ones you've given them?"

Daiki batted his eyelashes, like he'd seen Sage do during his vlogs, and smirked. "Whatever do you mean?"

Sage grinned at him.

Changing the subject, Daiki asked, "What do you want for dinner?"

"Everyone is going out tonight, but if you're not up to it, we can have a quiet night at home," Sage was quick to point out.

"Let's go to dinner but not out for the drinking Haru and Zen will most likely want to do." Sometimes life became the perfect storyboard. Daiki blinked to clear his watery eyes.

"What's wrong?" Sage swiped his fingers under Daiki's eyes.

"Nothing... everything is perfect. Would you help me hang something downstairs?"

"Um, sure." Sage followed Daiki back to the apartment.

Daiki slid a stack of canvases out from under the bed. He flipped through them until he came to the one he wanted.

Sage looked over his shoulder at it. "Is that us?"

"It was my fantasy of what I didn't think would ever happen." Daiki held out his painting of two men holding each other on a roof under a big moon.

"Your fantasy?" Sage asked.

"To have someone to share all the big and little things in life with. Someone to love."

Sage encircled him a tight hug. "Now that's our reality."

Epilogue

HARU WHISTLED. "So that's what a sold-out arena looks like at the end of summer concert season."

Sage trailed him back to the dressing room, feeling light-headed but kind of excited. "The training-wheel shows are over."

As they entered the dressing room, Wayuu asked Zen, "Where were you all day?"

"Trying to reproduce," Zen teased, then frowned. "Why?"

"Never mind." Wayuu stomped off to do his preshow jumps.

Why didn't Zen tell him the truth?

Daiki handed Sage his pill bottle. He took one and handed the bottle back. "Thanks."

"How are you feeling?" Daiki asked.

"There's about a billion people out there."

Chuckling, Daiki shook his head. "I doubt that, but it probably feels that way."

"This is a big show to have a screwup."

"It'll be okay," Daiki encouraged.

Sage took the blindfold Daiki held out to him. The fabric he used had gotten progressively more sheer, so he could see through the fabric when he wanted to. He had been experimenting with seeing the audience. "I don't know if I need it anymore, but it's legend."

Daiki grinned in that sexy almost-innocent way of his and said, "Maybe we can retire it to the bedroom."

Trying not to choke on Daiki's bold words, Sage asked, "Would you tie it on, later?"

"Of course."

Zen gathered the band. "Remember, whatever happens, happens. Let's show people how perfect their imperfections are. Kashi-sei on three."

THE SHOW had been going great until the song "Wabi-sabi." A power surge plunged the entire arena into darkness. The irony of the lyrics embodying the concept of embracing imperfections wasn't lost on Sage.

Sage's anxiety skyrocketed, and he had trouble catching his breath.

But out of the pitch-black, the lights of thousands of cell phones seeped through his blindfold. He pushed the fabric up onto his forehead.

The crowd picked up the words that had been lost to the dead mics and sang their hearts out.

Sage stepped from behind his drums to join his band at the edge of the stage.

Kashi-sei linked arms and let their fans serenade them with lyrics about happiness not being perfection but the ability to deal with and embrace their flaws.

Haru leaned in and shouted into Sage's ear, "Let this be proof. We're not just another boy band."

Author's Note

I WROTE many parts of *Not Another Boy Band* while on a three-week trip to Japan, which is why the story is set mostly in Tokyo and Kyoto. I was actually at the Inari shrine when enlightenment, shall we call it, about this story's resolution came to me.

The issues the main characters face—demonizing "the other," censorship, homophobia, transphobia, fear—are global issues. We all need to work together to eliminate these issues.

So why did I dedicate a book set in Japan to a Chinese novelist? Tianyi is now serving a ten-year prison term for writing homoerotic fiction. Censorship laws can be extremely strict, and only the brave dare to tread close to the line.

The result is that many voices are silenced out of fear. Visibility is a luxury not everyone can afford.

Why am I writing yet another story about a band? I've watched a number of musical groups implode over a hint of same-sex love. In the West, some of us celebrate out-and-proud rock stars, in part because it is still a rare event. We know many idols remain closeted for fear of losing their fan bases. I wanted to celebrate those who boldly tread across the notes and melodies to be exactly who they were born to be.

I truly believe seeing and understanding can lead to acceptance. This is why I write rainbow romance, and why Sage starts the band Kashi-sei.

I truly hope you enjoyed this adventure.

Be kind to yourself and others.

Many hugs & much love,

Z. Allora

Z. ALLORA didn't always believe in romance, although before giving up on happily ever afters completely, Z. took out a personal ad in a college newspaper. On October 20, 1987, at 5:08 p.m., Z. found what they didn't think existed—their other half. Five years later, Z. married their best friend and true love.

A bit of an overachiever, Z.'s earned three bachelor's degrees (psychology, English, and philosophy) and a master's degree in psychology. Z. loved enhancing the quality of life of people in their residential and day programs, but their love's job swept Z. to live in Singapore, Israel, and China. Much of Z.'s adult life has been spent traveling. So far Z. has played in thirty-four countries and can't wait to add to the list.

Z. believes each of us is wonderfully unique and deserving of a happily ever after. Regardless where we are on the infinite spectrum of gender identity or orientation, our differences and similarities should be both respected and celebrated.

Identifying as nonbinary of the transmasculine variety, Z.'s pronouns are they/them, though based on current gender constructs, Z. presents as female looking much of the time.

One of the biggest goals of Z.'s writing is to validate everyone's individual uniqueness. There's an infinite spectrum within each stripe of the rainbow and Z. wants to explore them all.

Z. will never apologize for having too much yaoified smexy goodness in their books. Z. teases that plot is simply the words between the sex scenes (though that's a bit of an exaggeration). Sex is one of our most important and basic forms of communication, and Z. feels it's a vital part of understanding her characters.

Z. Allora truly believes this rainbow romance is changing hearts and minds and will continue to speak out for love for all of us.

Email: Z.AlloraHappyEndings@gmail.com
Facebook: Z Allora Allora and join Z.'s Yaoified Love group (for fun, character chatters, giveaways, and silliness)
Website: www.zallorabooks.com
Blog: zallora.blogspot.com
Dreamspinner Press: www.dreamspinnerpress.com/books/z-allora-637-a

BENT
NOT
BROKEN

Z. ALLORA

Stefano Rossi longs for the mystical—and so far unattainable—peace of reaching subspace. But can he accept that the person who can take him there is a man?

Riku Tao has given up on finding a sub who complements him. He'll stick with doing demonstrations at the BDSM club the Edge. He certainly doesn't have time for a closeted Catholic guy with internalized biphobia… and yet he cannot help but want to protect Stefano and give him what he needs. A history of physical and sexual abuse makes it impossible for Stefano to come out of the closet, and Riku certainly isn't going back in.

Perhaps an arrangement of six months to explore their desires will be enough to satisfy them both.

Or it might break their hearts.

To take hold of his future with the man he's coming to love, Stefano will need to move beyond the pain of his past, and he won't be able to do it alone.

www.dreamspinnerpress.com

THE
LONGEST
night

Z. ALLORA

The holiday season is lonely for construction worker Benjamin Morgan, a big muscular guy who just wants to submit, obey, and serve. But the men he's attracted to usually don't have a dominant bone in their bodies. He's done seeking his BDSM dreams with someone who isn't interested in putting him in his rightful place—on his knees at their feet.

When a friend sets up a meeting with Foster Ridgeway at the BDSM club, Entwined, Benjamin has his doubts. Of course he is attracted to bookish Foster, who works for the same construction company, but how will someone so small and delicate-looking master Benjamin? But when Foster—the tiny temple of dominance wielding a crop—heads toward Benjamin, he might get what he's always wanted, just in time for Solstice.

ROCKING THIN ICE

Z. ALLORA

Can a sexy rock star show a relationship-phobic ice skater that there's more to life than gold medals?

When ice-skating's bad boy Blaze first glimpses Drake, every fantasy he's ever had flares to life. Not only is rock star Drake sexy as sin, his songs awaken a longing in Blaze that he's denied for years. But Blaze Parker doesn't believe in relationships—at least not those that last more than twenty minutes.

Drake Keys has dreamed about the sensual ice skater for years. When Drake is kicked out of his band because of his bisexuality, he drives across the country to finally see the man he's had a crush on skate live.

Though the attraction is instant and intense, both Blaze and Drake have baggage that puts any relationship on thin ice. Blaze is driven by a long-ago betrayal to prove himself a champion, and Drake, uncertain about the future, hopes to resurrect his music career. As they take a road trip together, Drake romances Blaze, hoping to melt his heart and show him that love is possible… but not without some tough decisions.

www.dreampsinnerpress.com

www.ingramcontent.com/pod-product-compliance
Lightning Source LLC
Chambersburg PA
CBHW060100260626
47160CB00005B/1739